WITCHING FOR MOXIE

PREMONITION POINTE, BOOK 5

DEANNA CHASE

Copyright © 2021 by Deanna Chase

Editing: Angie Ramey

Cover image: © Ravven

ISBN print: 978-1-953422-14-9

This book is a work of fiction. Names, characters, places, and incidents are products of the author's imagination or are used fictitiously. Any resemblance to actual events, locals, business establishments, or persons, living or dead, are entirely coincidental.

Bayou Moon Press, LLC

www.deannachase.com

Printed in the United States of America

ABOUT THIS BOOK

Iris Hartsen thought she'd finally gotten everything she'd ever wanted. She had her dream job of mayor of Premonition Pointe and was married to a handsome, charismatic man who adored her. But after finding out her husband was involved with a local drug dealer, she suddenly found herself single and forced to step down as mayor. Now she's starting over. But when a curse hits Premonition Pointe and tourism dries up, turning the beach town into a ghost town, Iris will do anything to save the village she loves, even if it means leaning on a new man in her life. With the help of the local coven and a too-good-too-be-true neighbor, Iris's new beginning means tapping into magic she didn't know she had and maybe even learning to trust again.

CHAPTER ONE

"*C*an you feel the magic prickling over your skin?" Iris Hartsen asked the four coven members who were standing with her in the empty town square. Less than an hour ago, some sort of curse had been cast that had rendered Premonition Pointe a ghost town. Normally the beachside town would be bustling with tourists for the summer, but the shops were eerily empty after all the out-of-towners had mysteriously disappeared.

Grace Valentine, a local realtor, tucked a stray lock of auburn hair behind her ear and shook her head. "No. I don't feel anything at all." She turned to her friends. "Do any of you?"

Hope and Joy both said no, but Gigi nodded.

"I feel… something. Like the air is charged maybe?" Gigi, a pretty blonde, ran her right hand down her left arm and made a face. "It's kind of sticky, like humidity only…" She rubbed her arm again and winced. "That wasn't pleasant."

"It stings a little bit," Iris said, frowning. "I wonder why it only affects the two of us."

"It must be the type of magic," Joy said, scrolling through

1

her smartphone. "It says here that if herbs are the primary source of a curse, then witches who are skilled in earth magic are more likely to be affected."

"You work with herbs?" Gigi asked Iris, her eyes alight with interest. Gigi had a new skincare line that she sold through a local shop and was becoming quite well-known for her skills with plants.

"No," Iris said, shaking her head. "I don't at all. Or at least I haven't in the past." Iris came from a long line of powerful witches, but she'd never been especially magical herself. Her mother had gotten her power from the ocean, and had been the type of witch who knew things before they happened. She'd also had spirit guides, but Iris hadn't shared her gifts. The only ability Iris thought she'd had was an uncanny sense for business. She could predict with almost certain accuracy when a business would thrive and when it wouldn't. It was always a shame when new business owners in Premonition Pointe disregarded her advice. Though no one would be consulting her now since she'd been ousted as mayor a few days ago.

Gigi placed a light hand on Iris's arm. "I would be happy to work with you if you want to test out some potions or herbal concoctions."

"That's very kind of you," Iris said, smiling at the other woman as a small weight lifted off her heart. As the longtime mayor of Premonition Pointe, Iris had found herself too busy to make or maintain many friendships. It was one of her major regrets in the life that she'd built for herself. But given the chance, she'd love to try to rectify that oversight now that she was going to have a lot more free time on her hands. And she could think of no better group of women than the four standing with her in the town square.

"Thank you, Gigi. I'd love to take you up on that offer sometime," Iris said with a hand over her heart. "But right now, I think I better head over to the new interim mayor's office and let him know your suspicions so that maybe they can narrow down the hunt for who did this and why."

"We'll go with you," Joy said quickly, her gaze shifting from Iris to her friends and back again. "I know Tad from the Arts Council and…"

"And what?" Iris asked after a beat.

"Um, how well do you know Tad?" Joy asked.

Iris shook her head. "I don't. Not really. The most interaction I've had with him was while standing in line at the Bird's Eye Bakery yesterday. He asked me a few questions about the city budget, and when I said I'd be happy to go over it with him, he declined. He said he'd figure it out." Iris frowned and then sighed. "I guess he was worried about how it would look to the council if the ousted mayor was in the office. What do they think? That I'm going to sabotage things now that I'm not running the show? The only thing I've ever wanted for Premonition Pointe was for it to be a success." She glanced around at the empty streets that should be bustling with people, and her heart sank. "Now look at it."

Joy placed a light hand on her arm. "We know you only want what's best for Premonition Pointe. That's why you came to us immediately after this curse hit the town, right?"

Iris nodded.

"Exactly," Joy said. "That's why we'll go with you to the mayor's office. From my experience, Tad has a chip on his shoulder and isn't likely to accept our help, but I've kind of figured out how to finesse him. If you don't mind, I'd like a chance to see if I can get through to him before he dismisses us outright."

"Yeah. Okay." A pit of unease formed in Iris's gut. This wasn't going to go well. There was no question about it. Joy's assessment of the man lined up with Iris's first impression of him when she'd met him at the bakery. He'd been defensive and acted as if he was threatened by Iris's offer to counsel him. She'd shrugged it off, but now that there was serious trouble in Premonition Pointe, how could she leave her beloved town in the hands of a man who seemed too ego-driven to accept help? She doubted they'd be successful in convincing him of their theory, but they had to try. She nodded to Joy. "Lead on."

Joy straightened her shoulders and strode down Main Street, straight toward the city offices. Iris trailed behind, knowing that if she was in front of the pack, it wouldn't help matters. But everything inside of her longed to take control, to be the one who dealt with the city's crisis just as she had countless times before when something went wrong in her beachside town.

"It sucks what happened to you," Hope said, falling into step beside Iris. "I heard they ousted you because of your ex."

Iris nodded. "Yep. Or at least that was the most convenient excuse."

Hope let out a growl. "The mediocre men strike again. Pushing a strong, smart woman out so one of them can be installed into a position of power. Disgusting if you ask me."

"It is. But it's done, and I'm moving on. Or at least I was trying to before *this* happened." There was no arguing Hope's assessment. It was exactly what had happened, but if Iris spent too much time dwelling on it, she was going to turn into a bitter bitch. Instead, she was determined to move forward, to find a way to help Premonition Pointe grow and thrive without being the mayor. Though, that wasn't something she could do if the town was cursed.

"We'll figure it out." Hope squeezed her hand and gave her a reassuring smile. "If there is one thing we girls have, it's tenacity."

"That's why I came to the coven." Iris returned the squeeze, and for the first time in months, she felt like she wasn't alone. Why hadn't she befriended these women before? She'd always liked them. The problem had been time. Iris had poured everything she had into her job. One good thing about being fired was that time would no longer be an issue. Or at least not for the next few months before she had to find another job.

Iris's heart started to race as they neared the city offices. The overwhelming feeling of failure settled over her. The humiliation of being fired was something she'd firmly buried deep down, determined to ignore it. She knew she'd been a damned good mayor. No one could seriously argue that the town hadn't flourished under her leadership. She sucked in a deep, steadying breath and followed Hope into the offices.

Chaos reigned.

"Julie! I told you to get the governor on the line! If you can't do your damned job, then just get the hell out of here!" Tad barked from his office.

Julie had tears streaming down her face as she frantically dialed and then redialed a number with shaky fingers.

Anger seized Iris as she watched her former assistant's hands shake.

After another unsuccessful phone call, Julie put the phone back down on the receiver and winced as she said, "He's on his way to Washington, Mr. Howell. His assistant says he won't be available until tomorrow."

"That's *Mayor* Howell. And this can't wait until tomorrow!" Tad barged out of his office, red-faced with his lips twisted into a scowl. He was wearing an expensive suit and had his hair slicked back with too much hair product. "We need him to call in the Magical Task Force so we can get to the bottom of this. Don't you understand anything?"

"I tried, Mayor Howell." Julie straightened her shoulders and turned to him, her head held high, though there was no mistaking the tremor in her voice. "No one else has the clearance to authorize the task force."

Tad let out a growl and started to stalk toward her.

Iris's instincts took over, and she started to move forward, intending to cut him off before he reached Julie. But Joy put her arm out, stopping her, and said, "We can help."

The mayor jerked to a stop and turned to her, his expression full of surprise. Clearly, he hadn't realized they were there. His gaze swept over them, and then his eyes narrowed when he spotted Iris. "What are you doing here?"

"We came to offer help," Joy said before Iris could answer. "The town has been cursed, and we think—"

"I don't give a flying fuck what you think." He pointed to the door. "Get out. We're in a crisis, and the last thing I need is a bunch of middle-aged busybodies getting in the way."

"Well that was rude," Hope said, placing her hands on her hips. "If you'd get out of your own way for two seconds, we could—"

"Leave now!" He barked. "And stay out of my way unless you want the sheriff to show up on your doorstep."

Iris was fuming at Tad's dismissal. Clearly, the man had no idea how to do anything, and he was acting as if she and the coven were amateur Scooby Doos instead of powerful witches with resources at their fingertips. Without a word, she walked over to Julie, picked up the phone, and dialed the personal cell number of the governor's assistant.

"Iris Hartsen, hang up that phone, or I'll have you arrested just as soon as the boys in blue get here," Tad said through clenched teeth.

"Lisbeth?" Iris said into the phone, completely ignoring Tad's temper tantrum. "It's Iris Hartsen over here in Premonition Pointe. It appears the town has been cursed, and our new mayor, Tad Howell, is requesting an emergency dispatch of the Magical Task Force. Unfortunately, we haven't been able to get ahold of the governor. Can you help us out?" After Iris answered a few questions about the curse and the state of the town, she let out a sigh of relief when Lisbeth told her she'd do her best to reach the governor.

Tad's nostrils flared, but for once he kept his mouth shut.

"Thanks, Lisbeth. You're the best." Iris placed the handset back on the phone base and turned to look Tad in the eye. "That was the governor's personal assistant. She said she's sending him the paperwork immediately and as soon as the request is approved, you'll receive a fax."

"When will that be?" Tad demanded.

Iris shrugged. "Later this afternoon or maybe first thing in the morning would be my guess. But from personal experience, I expect that you won't see anyone from the task force for at least a few days. There just aren't enough agents to cover all the emergencies in the state. And since no one appears to be physically hurt, we won't be first on the list."

"Well, that wasn't all that useful then, was it? No wonder the city council threw your ass out." He turned on his heel, stalked back into his office, and slammed the door.

CHAPTER TWO

"*H*e's a right asshole, isn't he?" Hope said, not bothering to lower her voice.

"There's no question about that," Iris agreed, already pulling the door open. Their visit to the mayor had been a complete waste of time.

"Iris?" Julie called.

With her hand still clutching the door, Iris froze and glanced over her shoulder at her former assistant. "Yes, Julie?"

The younger woman glanced briefly at her boss's door before looking back at Iris. Her cheeks flushed pink as she said, "It hasn't been the same without you around here."

Some of the anger coiling in Iris's gut dissipated as she gave the younger woman a grateful smile. "Thank you for saying that. I wish things had ended up differently."

"Me too." Julie ran out from behind her desk and wrapped her arms around Iris, holding on tightly.

Iris was too stunned at first to move but then returned the embrace and blinked back the sting of tears. She and Julie hadn't really been close. They'd had a good working relationship, but there hadn't exactly been a friendship between the two women. So the blatant display of emotion was a surprise, but she welcomed it, pleased to know she'd had some sort of effect on the other woman. "It'll be all right, Julie. I promise."

Julie stepped back, her expression skeptical, but she still nodded. "Thank you for your help."

"Any time, all right?" Iris squeezed her hand and lowered her voice. "You have my number. Use it if you need to."

"Okay," Julie whispered back and then returned to her desk.

"Let's go," Iris said and strode out of the office feeling sick to her stomach. The situation in the mayor's office was worse than she'd anticipated. But there wasn't anything she could do. Was there?

"We should still do the spell to see if we can figure out the origin of the curse," Grace said, staring out at the ocean. The wind had picked up, blowing her hair into her face, and when she brushed it back, she was frowning and her eyes were troubled. "How much experience do you have with the Magical Task Force?"

"Not much," Iris admitted. "They are stretched thin and usually are only deployed when magic is used as a weapon against people. Unless we find out that the tourists were hurt or missing, they likely won't spend much time here."

"It's settled then," Grace said, straightening her shoulders and walking toward her car. "We'll do the spell ourselves and see if we can trace and reverse this curse. Let's go. We have work to do."

Iris stared in awe as the four women fanned out, each heading for their vehicles. Their determination and unquestioning resolve to help touched her heart and had her scrambling after Grace and into the passenger seat. "Thank you for... everything."

"There's nothing to thank me for," she said. "This is our town, too. We love it here, and there's no way we're going to let whoever did this get away with it."

The fierceness in her tone filled Iris with hope as they sped down the empty streets.

Ten minutes later, the five women were gathered around a firepit on the windy bluff above the Pacific Ocean. Gigi opened a canvas bag and started pulling out a mortar and pestle while Hope made a circle with salt and Grace placed five candles around the firepit.

Joy turned to Iris. "Have you ever done this before?"

"Tried to trace a curse?" Iris asked, frowning. "No, nothing like that."

"I meant combine your power with that of other witches," Joy said.

"Oh. No. I haven't done that either." The truth was, Iris had only worked with her own mother, trying water spells and searching for spirit guides. She'd never been very good at either.

"Well then, it looks like you're in for a bit of a wild ride." She smiled at Iris and tugged her over to a log that had been carved into a bench. "You sit here."

Iris studied the log. It was gorgeous with a natural finish and looked like something that belonged in Lucas King's showroom instead of outside on a deserted bluff. "Did Lucas make this?" Iris asked Hope.

"Yep. There's two more coming when he has time. Isn't it wonderful?" Hope put the salt container back in Gigi's bag and moved to sit next to Iris. "He said he didn't want us to have to get mud stains on our clothes every time we had a coven meeting, so he started working on these. He's a sweetheart of a man, especially since he doesn't really have time to be doing side projects like this."

"It's a labor of love, I'm sure," Iris said, tamping down the surprising jab of jealousy that jolted through her. It wasn't that Iris had her sights on Hope's fiancé. No, that wasn't it at all, but she was envious of their relationship. Even though she'd thought herself happy with Tom before he'd proven to be a low-life, he'd never really worried about Iris's needs. He wasn't the type to surprise her with gifts or take it upon himself to do anything to make her life easier. She'd had her chores and he'd had his. And that was that. Sex on Wednesdays. Dinner out on Sunday. One week-long vacation to the locale of Tom's choice every year. And that was pretty much the basis of their relationship.

Damned if that wasn't sad. How had she gotten to the point of believing that they'd been happy? She'd put all of her effort into work, and Tom... Well, even though he'd had a successful lumber business, he'd gotten involved with drug dealers for reasons she still didn't understand.

Last she'd heard, Tom had sold his lumber business and opened an art gallery in a smaller town about thirty miles south of Premonition Pointe. He also had a younger girlfriend who was some sort of psychic palm reader. Every time she thought of him, her gut churned, and she had to stop herself from ordering a curse that caused erectile dysfunction and butt acne. The jackass had evaded any sort of charges related to the drug trafficking due to some technicality, and he had reinvented himself with a new and improved life. Meanwhile, Iris was out of a job, and more importantly, it had been a job she'd loved. And every bit of it was Tom's fault.

"Okay, let's get this show on the road," Grace said, taking a seat on a rough log across from them. Joy and Gigi followed, filling out a circle around the firepit. White pillar candles had been placed in front of each of them, and Gigi was busy dumping a handful of herbs into her mortar.

Gigi turned to Iris. "Can you feel the stickiness already intensifying?"

Iris nodded. Her skin was starting to tingle uncomfortably from the magic in the air.

"It's because we're working on the tracing spell. It knows," Gigi said and thinned her lips into a straight line.

"How?" Iris peered into the mortar. It was a mix of bright red and yellow with a pile of green herbs.

"It's the hibiscus," she said solemnly. "I use it in most of my divination spells."

"But you haven't done anything yet," Iris said, confused about how just the petals of a hibiscus plant could affect the spell blanketing the town.

"I didn't have to. My years of working with hibiscus in divination spellcasting has caused my magic to sort of go on autopilot. The moment I crushed them up, the spell responded, ready to spill its secrets." Gigi reached for Iris's hand and placed a small number of crushed petals into her palm. "Feel anything different?"

The sticky magic intensified, causing Iris's skin to crawl. She immediately dumped the contents of her hand into the firepit and rubbed her palm on her jeans. "That was... intense."

Gigi nodded. "It's because of the type of spell. If it's too much, you don't have to be a part of this."

Iris shook her head. No way was she sitting this out. It was the first time she'd ever really experienced what it was like to have magical powers. In all of her forty-seven years on Earth, she'd always assumed that she'd been skipped over in the magic department. But now, all of that had changed. If she could help Gigi and the coven discover where the curse came from, she was all in. "No. I want to help. Let's do this. Just let me know what I need to do."

"Okay." Gigi handed Iris the mortar and a clump of dandelions. "Pull the blooms off and drop them into the mortar. Once that's done, use the pestle and crush them together with the hibiscus."

"I'm on it." Iris closed her fingers over one of the dandelion blooms and bit back a wince when her fingers burned from the contact. That just meant that her magic was reacting to the dandelion, right? As she crushed the blooms with the pieces already in the mortar, her blood pressure spiked, and her vision blurred. She expected to be swamped with dizziness, but instead, her vision cleared and suddenly she was standing in her backyard watching as someone in a black cloak lit a fire in a chalice. The person raised their arms and then chanted an incantation, causing the fire to shoot up into the air. A bolt of lightning crackled through the blue sky, hitting the chalice and shattering it into tiny pieces that scattered all over the yard.

"Iris?" Gigi called. "Hey, are you all right?"

The voice seemed far away, and it wasn't until Gigi called her name again that Iris blinked rapidly and found herself back on the bluff with the coven members all staring at her expectantly.

Iris glanced around at the other four women and then down at the pillar candles that were all lit, their flames swaying in the breeze.

"What just happened there?" Gigi asked, her brow furrowed.

Iris didn't know what to make of her vision. Was it some sort of dream? A real vision? She'd never experienced anything like that before. She took in Gigi standing across from her. Gigi's white linen skirt and matching peasant blouse flared out behind her in the wind as her honey-blond hair whipped around her face. She looked ethereal and powerful and like everything Iris had ever wanted to be when she was younger.

"Iris?" Gigi asked. "What did you see?"

"How did you know I saw something?" Iris asked, still disoriented.

"I recognize the signs. You were here physically, but you were fixated on something none of the rest of us could see." Gigi lowered her voice as she added, "My mom used to do that every once in a while."

The pain in Gigi's voice touched something deep inside of Iris. She knew that Gigi had lost her mother when she was just a teenager, and while Iris hadn't gone through anything remotely as traumatic, she knew what it was like to go through life at that age without her own mother. Except Iris's mom had left voluntarily. A sharp jab of pain stabbed Iris's heart, but she ignored it and said, "I did see something, or someone, doing a spell in my backyard, but I don't know if it was real."

Gigi's eyes widened. "In your backyard? Do you think it was the curse?"

Iris nodded. "Yes. In my vision it was, but how do I know if it really happened?"

"Let's find out," Grace said, holding her hands out to the side, indicating she wanted everyone to join hands.

Iris linked hands with Hope and Grace. Immediately the

intensity of the sticky magic faded, making Iris feel almost normal. "Whoa."

"It's fascinating, right?" Gigi asked, holding Iris's gaze.

Iris frowned. The magic was all but gone, leaving her feeling both at a loss and also freer. She wasn't at all sure she liked it. After years of thinking she wasn't magical, she wasn't quite ready to lose her connection to her power. "Won't holding hands like this block everything out?"

"This will help us focus. It's all still there," Gigi said. "Trust me."

Iris nodded, hoping she was right.

Gigi closed her eyes and started an incantation. "Salt and sea, wind and fire, show us what the earth has transpired."

The other three witches repeated the words, and when they repeated the chant a third time, Iris joined in. A zap of electricity sparked through Iris's fingertips and shot through her veins. The more they chanted, the more intense the electrical charge became, until Iris was vibrating with it. The magic that had been coating her skin was back, but this time it felt like a comforting blanket rather than an irritation.

The flames lighting the candles turned blue just before smoke filled the air within their circle and then came together into a solid form to act out the exact scene Iris had witnessed in her vision.

The smoke dissipated just as quickly as it appeared, and once it was gone, silence descended upon the small group of witches.

Iris pulled away from Grace and Hope, immediately regretting it when her skin started to itch with the magic of the curse. She wrapped her arms around herself, trying to block it out, but that was a useless endeavor.

"That's what you saw in your vision, isn't it?" Gigi asked.

Iris nodded. "Exactly, only I saw it happen in my backyard instead of right here on the bluff."

"Damn," Hope muttered, running a hand through her dark hair. "This really isn't good."

"No. It isn't," Iris said, her stomach roiling at the implications.

"We need someone with a motive. It's the only way to keep them from suspecting you," Gigi said.

"Who has it out for you, Iris?" Joy asked. "Any enemies?"

"You mean besides the new mayor, my ex, and most of the city council? Not to mention any number of disgruntled citizens who weren't fans of some city policy over the last handful of years?" Iris threw her hands up. "The list is endless."

Grace gave her a sympathetic nod and opened her mouth to say something, but she was cut off by the sound of sirens.

They all turned to find a patrol car parked at the curb with another one jerking to a stop right behind it.

Iris watched as John Garrison, a veteran officer in the Premonition Pointe police department, strode toward her with his handcuffs in one hand. When he reached her, he was all business as he said, "Iris Hartsen, you're under arrest for casting an illegal spell over the town of Premonition Pointe and for trying to cover it up with witchcraft."

"What?" Iris yelped, but then clamped her mouth shut as John started to recite her Miranda rights.

"You can't arrest her," Gigi demanded. "You have no idea what you're talking about."

Hope, Joy, and Grace chimed in, defending Iris without hesitation.

Iris appreciated it more than they could possibly know, but the truth was, if someone had cast the curse from her backyard and the authorities had figured that out, Iris was now their number-one suspect. The best thing she could do at that point was to cooperate and find a lawyer. She glanced at Gigi. "Is Sebastian in town?"

"Yeah," Gigi said, already pulling her phone out of her skirt pocket. "I'll have him meet you at the station."

"Thanks," Iris said and let John escort her to his vehicle.

CHAPTER THREE

*I*ris sat on the cold metal bench in her cell and stared at the concrete walls, wondering how her life had spiraled so far out of control. Divorced. Unemployed. Accused of cursing her beloved town. The worst part was, if her vision and the divination spell were correct, then law enforcement likely already had evidence.

Was this really how she was going to go down? A curse that ruined everything she'd worked for over the last several years? Angry tears stung her eyes, but she blinked them back, too enraged to let anyone in the police station see her weakness. Despite whatever evidence they'd collected, she'd be fighting the charges until the bitter end. If there was one thing Iris had going for her, it was moxie. That's what her father had said even when she was a little girl. She'd proved him right numerous times, and this would be no different. Once Sebastian worked his magic and got her bail set, she'd do whatever it took to figure out who'd framed her and bring them to their knees. They'd rue the day they messed with Iris Hartsen.

"I gotta say, this isn't how I saw things playing out," a familiar and unwelcome voice said from outside her cell.

Iris jumped up off her bench and strode over to the cell door, peering through the bars at her ex. "Tom. What the hell are you doing here?"

He raised one bushy eyebrow. "Is that anyway to talk to the man who's going to make all of this go away for you?"

She nearly scoffed as she stared at him and took in his appearance. He was sporting a fake orange tan, and his hair was longer and shaggier than it used to be, as if he were going for an aging-surfer vibe. And to top off the look, he was wearing board shorts and a T-shirt that said *Hangin' Loose.* She shook her head, dying to tell him that he looked like a sad, older man who was desperate to relive his teenage years. Instead, she cocked her own eyebrow and met his gaze. "How exactly do you think you can help me?" A tiny bloom of hope sparked in her chest as she asked, " Do you know who really did this?"

"Oh, come on, Iris. Everyone knows it was you. They are scouring your property now for traces of the spell. Not to mention, you're the only one with a motive. Who else would even think of dispelling tourists after you were fired? No one knows better than you how important they are to the health of this town."

Iris gaped at him. "You can't be serious. You actually think I cast some sort of curse? Besides that whole idea being completely absurd, since when have I ever been magical?"

"You were arrested at the bluffs with the town coven, weren't you?" he asked, a smug look on his face. "You can't really use the ignorance excuse when you were doing some sort of séance. How do you think that will look to a jury?"

Why was he so damned smug? It was as if he was enjoying

the fact that she was the one behind bars this time. Iris wanted to reach through the bars of the cell and choke him. Not that she was a violent person, but she'd had one hell of a day. Instead, she sniffed and said, "I'm not even going to justify any of that with a response."

"Whatever you say, Iris." He narrowed his eyes, now glaring at her as he did nothing to hide his distaste. "It was always your way or the highway, wasn't it?"

"What the hell is that supposed to mean?" she asked in a low, shaky voice. "Did you really just come here to pick a fight with me?"

"Not exactly." He ran a hand through his too-long locks, smiling to himself before he sobered and stared her in the eye. "I'll admit I don't hate seeing you knocked down a peg or two. The self-righteous act you've been sporting the last few years was nauseating. It's not like you never bent the rules. But when someone else does it, they're trash, right, Iris?"

So that was what he wanted. To gloat and try to humiliate her because she'd dumped him the moment she found out he was helping process and distribute illegal drugs. "I'm not the one who was working with a drug dealer and supplying drugs that harmed people in this town. How dare you act like anything I've ever done is on par with your crimes."

"And yet, you're the one sitting in a jail cell," he said, smirking at her.

Pure hatred for the man made her clutch at the bars until her knuckles turned white. She decided it was a good thing that she was locked up at that moment, because if he'd said anything like that to her when she was free, she would've snapped. "I won't be here for long."

"You'll still have criminal charges hanging over your head," he said. "How's that going to work out for you? No city is going to hire or elect someone whose been accused of cursing a whole town. But if you want, I can help you out there."

Iris narrowed her eyes, studying him. He was up to something; she just had no idea what that could be. Why hadn't he just left her alone to live his new life with his new girlfriend? The truth was, Iris didn't miss him. She missed companionship and having someone to talk to everyday, but Tom specifically? No. She'd learned all too quickly that she hadn't actually been in love with him. They'd just been together for a long time and he'd been comfortable. It occurred to her that maybe that was part of his problem and why he was so angry at her. He wasn't a stupid man. It was likely he'd known that and resented her for it. She shook her head, dislodging her thoughts and focusing on his words. "You think you can help? You just said you liked seeing me in this jail cell. Why would you help me, and more importantly, how?"

"The why is easy. It doesn't do me any favors with my new community to have my ex-wife in jail. That doesn't look good, especially since rumors about the drug ring are still circulating. No one really knows the details, but they know I was initially a person of interest. If you're rotting in jail, it will only make people take a second look at what went down here in Premonition Pointe and how exactly my charges were dropped. That's not something I want or need right now. I'm sure you understand."

"Right," she said dryly. Since he'd literally ruined her career, she knew all too well how being associated with a criminal could really mess up one's life. Even if they were divorced. The only difference was that Iris wasn't guilty. Tom had been. "Go on then. How is it that you think you can help me?"

His lips curved up into a tight, almost evil grin. "Well, as it turns out, there's a reason I was released on a technicality other than complete incompetence."

Iris has suspected as much, but she hadn't been able to find anything definitive. Besides, she'd let the matter drop since Tom had agreed to leave town. The less talk of the scandal, the better. Or so she'd thought. Too bad it hadn't worked. "And?"

"It turns out that the DA still owes me a favor or two. He's willing to let you plead out on a claim that the curse was an accident if you agree to never run for office in Premonition Pointe again. There'll likely be some probation as part of the deal, but you won't have to serve time. And then when you've satisfied the terms, the record will be sealed. Just sign the confession, and he'll get the paperwork rolling."

"Plead out?" she parroted as she tried to wrap her brain around what had just happened. She'd only been sitting in the jail cell for an hour, maybe two at most. And already Tom was coming in, playing negotiator with some sort of plea deal, even before they took the time to question her. "This is a set up. They set me up and you're in on it." It wasn't a question. There was no other possibility.

Tom shrugged. "It turns out, I might owe the DA a favor or two myself. But that has nothing to do with the choices you're facing right now. Take the deal, Iris. Then leave Premonition Pointe. Go make a life for yourself somewhere else. Somewhere on the east coast or down south. Leave things here be and move on."

Iris ground her teeth together and shook her head.

"Now, don't be stubborn. At least think about it. The DA is going to present your lawyer with the offer. You'll have twenty-four hours to consider it before he takes it off the table." He shook his head and gave her an exasperated look.

"Look out for yourself for once, Iris. I'm begging you. You can't win this one."

Iris tilted her head to the side and eyed the man she'd been married to for over fifteen years. Then it was her turn to shake her head. "I can't believe I once thought you were a man of integrity. I guess I was too blind to see it, or maybe I just didn't want to, but there's always been an undercurrent of moral ambiguity, hasn't there?"

He rolled his eyes. "Everyone has moral ambiguity. One just needs to look hard enough to find the limits."

"I suppose that's true," Iris said, nodding. "But no one has to look very hard to find yours. Whatever the DA has on you, it must be a doozy to get you in here to try to do his bidding. It must suck to be his bitch," she said with a tiny evil grin of her own, knowing her words would slice him to the quick. Tom was a proud man and always had been. Implying that he was someone else's lapdog wasn't going to sit well with him.

"Go fuck yourself, Iris. I only came here to try to help you. What you do with the offer is completely up to you. But just remember that if I end up losing my gallery because of you, or if Kimmie is given any grief for dating the ex of Premonition Pointe's town psycho, I'll be back, and you'll have to deal with me instead of the DA. And I won't be as forgiving."

"Threats?" she shot back as he moved toward the door that led back to the front of the station. "Really, Tom? After everything you've done?"

He paused with his hand on the doorknob. Then he glanced back and said, "There's no loyalty between us. You made that perfectly clear when you threw me out the minute you found out about the lumberyard and the drugs. You never even once asked me to explain why I was involved. You didn't care. It was obvious all that mattered to you was your job. So don't act like I owe you anything now."

"You wanted me to ask you why? You were fucking the woman who was in charge of the entire operation!" she blurted, finally getting to the heart of what had hurt her the most.

"Was I?" he asked coldly. "I guess you'll never really know since you never bothered to ask me." Without another word, he strode through the door, leaving her in silence to try to wrap her head around everything he'd just said.

CHAPTER FOUR

*I*ris stood in the threshold of her front door and felt as if she'd been punched in the gut. The normally tidy living room had been ransacked. The cushions on her couch were scattered over broken glass and her displaced flower arrangement that had been on a table by the front window. All of the drawers of her credenza were open, and paperwork was scattered everywhere.

"Was this the work of the Premonition Pointe police department, or did someone break in?" Sebastian asked from over her shoulder.

Iris handed her lawyer the paperwork that had been taped to her door. It was a notice that her place had been searched. The warrant was attached and as far as Iris could tell, it had been a legal search. If she made a fuss, she could probably get some sort of settlement from the department for all the damage they'd done to her belongings, but she didn't have the mental ability to deal with documenting everything. All she wanted to do was put everything back together, curl up in her bed, and pretend the day had never happened.

"Bastards," Sebastian said.

She nodded and let out a sigh as she got to work cleaning up the mess.

Sebastian followed her into the room and said, "Where can I find a garbage bag and a broom?"

Iris clutched a couch cushion to her chest and stared at him for a moment before she found her voice again. "You don't need to help with this. I can manage."

"I know I don't have to, but I'm going to anyway," he said, a determined look on his face. He pulled out his phone and started taking pictures of the mess. "Besides, I want to document what they did here."

Right. That was a good idea. Iris nodded. "I'll get the broom and some garbage bags."

For the next couple of hours, Iris and Sebastian meticulously went through her house, taking pictures of everything and then putting it back together. The search team hadn't left one inch untouched. She wasn't surprised to see her underwear scattered all over her floor, but when she spotted the purple dildo right there in the middle of her bed, she let out a gasp and shoved Sebastian out of the room, slamming the door behind him.

"Iris, wait. I need pictures," he said through the door.

"Not of this," she said, her voice full of authority. Then her gazed narrowed on the sex toy, and her cheeks burned with heat. "For the love of desperate housewives everywhere!" she muttered as she scooped it up and shoved it back into her dresser. "Unbelievable." Iris shook her head and then covered her face with her hands. "You can come in now."

"Are you sure?" he asked skeptically.

"Yes." Iris sank onto her bed, feeling completely violated and defeated.

Sebastian poked his head in. His dark hair fell over one eye, and there was a smudge of blood on his shirt from a cut on his finger that he'd gotten while helping her clean up a broken vase. "Are you okay?"

"No, but I'll survive." She gave him a weak smile and rose from the bed. "I'm just tired. It's been a day."

He nodded. "Let me take some photos, and then I'll grab us some takeout. Do you think you're up to going over a few things while we eat?"

"Yeah, I can do that." She glanced at her bedroom and grimaced. "This is gonna be fun cleaning later."

"I'd offer to help, but..." He shrugged. "I imagine you'd rather do this room yourself."

Iris let out a huff of laughter. "You've got that right. I'll go order something while you get your photos. Burgers okay?"

"They're perfect." He placed a reassuring hand on her arm and added, "It's going to be okay, Iris. I promise."

She knew there was no way he could guarantee anything, but she appreciated the gesture, nonetheless. "Thanks."

Needing to get out of the house for a few minutes, Iris opted to pick up the order she'd placed. With the burgers and fries in a bag in one hand and a six pack of beer in the other, she made her way back up her walkway and wouldn't have even noticed her neighbor Kade if he hadn't called out to her.

"Hey, Iris. How'd it go with the coven?" Kade was standing on his porch, one hand on the railing as he smiled over at her.

The tall man with vibrant blue eyes looked gorgeous in the twilight. She realized she'd only met him that morning when they'd walked to the coffee shop, and suddenly Iris felt like the day had lasted a hundred years. "Um, okay, I guess. What happened after that is when things went to shit."

He frowned. "What do you mean?"

"I was arrested and accused of casting the curse." She gritted her teeth, hating that anyone would ever even think she could do such a thing.

"Well, obviously that's not true," he said immediately, his smile instantly becoming a frown.

Iris's eyebrows shot up. How was it that a man she'd just met believed her, but the law enforcement of the town she'd loved and served for so long had been happy to believe the worst of her? "What makes you so sure?"

His frown deepened. "Because I was with you when the curse was cast. And all you were doing was sipping coffee and making eyes at BeeBee." At the sound of her name, his small fluffy dog came barreling out of the house and skidded to a stop at his feet.

Iris felt a smile claim her lips as she eyed the sweet pup. Then his words sank in, and she let out a small gasp. Of course. Kade was her alibi. With everything that had happened over the course of the day, that fact had completely slipped her mind. She cleared her throat. "Um, do you mind coming over for a bit? My lawyer is here, and I know he'd love to hear that straight from you."

"Not at all." He glanced down at his pup. "Do you mind if this troublemaker joins us?"

"Mind? I insist." Iris let out a whistle and then said, "Come on BeeBee. Over here, sweetheart." The dog shot off Kade's porch and made a beeline for Iris.

Kade chuckled as he followed his dog. "She's a bit of an attention whore."

Iris crouched down and scratched the dog's ears. "I can see that. But it's cool." She cooed at the pup. "We're going to get along just fine, aren't we BeeBee?"

BeeBee wagged her tiny tail, making her entire body wiggle

with excitement.

Iris laughed and opened the door for her. "Come on in then. Dinner's getting cold." She looked up at Kade, who was standing right behind them. "Did you eat? I got burgers for me and Sebastian, but I can share mine if you're hungry."

He chuckled. "I'm fine. I had leftover pizza not long ago. But BeeBee might not let you off that easily. She might drool all over you until you give her a bite."

"Oh, you're that kind of pet owner, are you?" Iris teased as they moved into the house. "She trained you early to feed her scraps, didn't she?"

"Guilty." He gave her a sheepish smile and followed her into the kitchen where they found Sebastian at her breakfast table, scribbling on a legal pad.

Sebastian glanced up and blinked at Kade, appearing surprised to see him there. "Hello."

"Hey." Kade waved at him and then snapped his fingers. BeeBee immediately returned to his side and sat.

"You may be a pushover with the table scraps, but damn, you really did a hell of a job training her," Iris said.

Kade shrugged one shoulder. "She's a good dog."

"No doubt about that," Sebastian said, rising and holding his hand out to Kade. "I'm Sebastian Knight, Iris's lawyer. And you are?"

"Oops!" Iris gave Sebastian an apologetic smile. "This is Kade Carson, my new neighbor and my alibi for this morning. I figured you'd want to talk to him."

Kade shook Sebastian's hand. "Nice to meet you, man."

"You too." Sebastian released his hold and sat back in the chair, the tension gone from his face. "Alibi, huh? Well, that's good news. Have a seat and let's get to work."

Two decimated burgers and an empty six pack of beer later,

Sebastian packed up his notes and stood. "I can't promise anything, but with Kade's statement that you were with him this morning as well as the bankcard charge record at the café, it should be enough to get these charges dropped. As long as they didn't uncover any evidence that can directly implicate you, their case has already fallen apart. I'll talk to the DA tomorrow and let you know where we stand."

Iris should have felt relief. She did have an alibi and records to back up her story, but who knew what had happened during the search? What if they'd planted evidence? Or if she had something in her home that they could somehow connect to the spell? Her thoughts raced, and her anxiety was at an all-time high, making her fidget in her chair.

Sebastian placed a hand on her shoulder. "Try to relax. They don't have anything that's going to hold up in court that we know about, and with this information, it's even worse. Let me do the worrying, all right?"

Iris blew out a breath. "Yeah, okay. Thanks."

He nodded and started to move toward the door.

"Sebastian?" she called after him. When he turned around, she added, "Tell Gigi thanks for everything."

"I will."

After her lawyer disappeared out the front door, Iris crossed her arms over the table and dropped her head so that her forehead was resting on her forearms. "I can't believe any of this happened."

"I can," Kade said.

She jerked her head back up and peered at him. "You can? Why?"

He frowned, and then his eyes hardened as he said, "Let's just say this isn't the first time that Tad Howell has had to deal with a cursed city."

CHAPTER FIVE

*I*ris let out a gasp as she studied the stormy-eyed man sitting next to her. "Do you know Tad?"

"I did a long time ago," he said as he picked up BeeBee and set her on his lap.

"What does that mean?" Iris asked, holding his gaze.

"We went to boarding school together for a few years." He ran his hand over his dog's back as his lips curved into a frown. "We were minors, so likely any of the records are sealed, but I know for a fact that he was involved in a curse in our sleepy New England town. Can you believe he had the nerve to blame it on the ghosts of the Salem witch trials?"

"You mean the ones that got away?" Iris asked, referring to the fact that all the actual witches that were to be burned at the stake had disappeared before the flames could get to them. It was rumored that they'd disguised themselves as men and lived long, secretive lives.

"Yep. He's not the brightest bulb in the box. Anyway, he did it to impress a girl, thinking that when he cleared it up, he'd be the hero. Only she knew all along that he'd been the one responsible and refused to give him the time of day."

"And how did she know?" Iris asked, intrigued by this information. Tad hadn't been in Premonition Pointe all that long. Four or five years at the most. As far as she knew, no one really knew the details of his past that far back. He had the right education, and with the ability to kiss ass, he'd finally gotten what he wanted. Her job. It was no wonder the city council wanted him instead of Iris. She didn't take orders well. Mr. Likes-to-curse-everyone seemed like the perfect lackey for anyone wanting to create issues.

"I might have told her," he said with a sheepish grin.

"Because you wanted to date her?" Iris guessed.

He chuckled. "Everyone wanted to date her. You don't think he'd get someone to cast a curse like that for just anyone, do you?"

"So he didn't do it himself?" Iris asked, trying to piece together what had happened all those years ago at their boarding school.

"No." Kade shook his head. "He's not that talented."

"So who did?" she asked.

"No idea. We never did find out. That was the one thing he wouldn't give up. He pled out so he wouldn't have to rat on his accomplice. I guess there really is honor among criminals sometimes."

Iris slumped. "That doesn't actually help me much if we don't know who he gets to do his bidding."

"Really? I figured it'd give you something to look for when we tail him in the morning."

Iris stared at him, her mouth open in surprise. "You want to tail the new mayor on the off chance that he leads us to his curse casters?"

He leaned forward, staring at her intently. "No. I mean yes. I doubt he's dumb enough to lead us straight to them, but whatever he does, it could lead to a clue or pattern or something that will help us figure out his motives. If we're lucky, he'll be careless enough that we'll piece together who did this. Because I already know it wasn't you or the coven of Premonition Pointe."

Iris sat back in her chair and crossed her arms over her chest. She desperately wanted to believe that he was on to something, but her skepticism was too strong. "How is it that you just happened to move to the same town as Tad Howell? Is this a setup of some sort?"

He let out a snort of humorless laughter. "Set up? I just gave your lawyer your alibi. Why would I be trying to set you up? I just met you this morning."

Iris raised one eyebrow. "You tell me. It's no secret that Tad and my ex are trying to run me out of town. Maybe you're part of the plan. You both went to a boarding school in New England and somehow managed to end up here all these years later?" Iris said. "That seems weird, doesn't it?"

"First of all, it's not that strange that Tad and I are both in Premonition Pointe. Our families both lived about forty-five miles inland from here. Our boarding school was connected to our church. That's why it was so shocking that he was involved in an actual curse. Good church boys aren't supposed to get into that kind of trouble. And second, I didn't know your ex wants you to leave," he said, his brows furrowed as if he were trying to put something together. "Why?"

"I have no idea. It's possible he just wants to hurt me. He knows how much I love this town. Or maybe the DA was forcing him to try to get me to leave. It's anyone's guess."

"Why is everyone so hell-bent on running you out of

town?" he asked, though he seemed to be talking to himself rather than expecting her to answer.

"I'm not real loved around here these days," Iris said with a smirk as if that wasn't an understatement. "But I don't think they just want me out because they don't like me. No, it's that they know I'll do whatever it takes to keep crime out of this town. Mayor or not, I won't let them get away with selling drugs, or trafficking stolen goods, or worse. I'll make it my mission to sniff them out and send them to jail."

"You could do that without being mayor?" he asked skeptically.

"Hell yes, I can," she said with authority. "I have contacts all over the state and enough community informants that when something hits the fan, I have people who will talk. Well, probably, but nothing is certain with all this fuckery. But Tad doesn't have that kind of network. At least not yet. The man is flailing and will be ousted soon enough. Premonition Pointe won't put up with incompetence long."

"Damn, Iris. You sound badass." He winked at her. "To answer your question, I didn't know that Tad lived here in Premonition Pointe, much less that he was the mayor when I decided to move here. That's a complete coincidence. I swear." He held his hand up in a three-finger salute. "Scout's honor."

She chuckled and shook her head slightly. "Okay, if that's true, then did you come here for a job or just to soak in the sea breezes?"

"Both? I'm working for Lucas King making custom furniture."

"You are?" Iris asked in disbelief. "He actually hired someone to help with his handmade line?"

Kade nodded. "Yep. I start tomorrow." He glanced at the

clock on the wall and grimaced. "It's getting late. Looks like I better call it a night. Will you be okay here by yourself?"

"I'll be fine," she said quickly, not wanting him to notice the panic building in her chest. The truth was, after her house had been searched, she wasn't feeling comfortable at all. What if they'd bugged it with mics, or worse, installed hidden cameras? If Tad was determined to get rid of her, blackmail videos were probably a pretty effective way to do it.

"All right then," Kade said as he stood, clutching BeeBee to his chest. "Be ready by six-thirty. We'll check in on Tad before I head over to Lucas's place. He has an appointment in the morning and wants me to meet him there by noon."

"So we're really going to do this, huh?" Iris asked. "Follow Tad around and see what he's up to?"

"Yep. Are you up for it?" he asked, a challenge in his tone.

"Definitely." Iris walked him to the door.

Once he was standing outside, he turned to her and opened his mouth as if he wanted to say something but then shut it and gave his head a tiny shake.

"What?" she asked.

"Nothing. Just… Take care tonight and don't hesitate to let me know if you need anything."

"What could I possibly need?" Besides someone to sit with her and keep her company so that she didn't feel quite so alone and vulnerable. Iris had always been independent. Even when she'd been married to Tom. She'd prided herself on being strong and capable. But after being arrested and accused of a crime and then coming home to a trashed house, she was having a little bit of trouble holding onto her bravado. She just hoped it didn't show.

"A friend?" he asked.

Dammit. Tears stung the backs of her eyes, but she refused

to let them show. Not now. She would not break down in front of her handsome neighbor. "I have friends," she lied. "I'll be fine."

He eyed her for a long moment and then nodded. "I'm sure you will, but I'm still right next door if you need anything. Anything at all. Okay?"

She nodded, touched by the sincerity in his tone. "Thanks." Her voice was huskier than she would have liked, but she continued anyway. "I really appreciate your help. It means a lot."

His lips curved into a smile that made her a little gooey inside. "You're welcome. Any enemy of Tad's is a friend of mine." He winked and then, with BeeBee in his arms, they returned to his house next door. Iris waited until the lights came on in his little cottage before she slipped back in and bolted the door behind her.

Iris glanced around, eyeing her space, looking for anything that might be out of place or, more importantly since the house had been tossed, anything that appeared to have not moved. Surely anything they'd bugged they'd want to make sure it didn't get swept up in the cleanup. Right?

Her pulse quickened and she moved toward a framed print hanging on the wall. After running her fingers all around the edges and finding nothing, she turned her attention to a wall-mounted metal sculpture that read *Beach Babes*. It wasn't something that Iris would've picked out herself, but it had been a gift from her mother when Iris and Tom had purchased the place ten years ago. At the time, she'd felt obligated to hang it just to keep the peace between them. Now that she and her mother weren't exactly on speaking terms, she'd contemplated taking it down, but something always stopped her.

Iris spent the next forty-five minutes inspecting her house

for bugs or video surveillance, but didn't find anything obvious. She wondered if she should call in a professional investigator or if she was just being paranoid. After the day's events, she decided paranoid was better than being framed.

Who should she call? She didn't want to pick just anyone. It should be someone who was trusted. Sebastian would know. She pulled out her phone and called him.

"Iris, how are you doing?" a woman asked.

"Um, did I call the right number? I'm looking for Sebastian Knight."

"Oh. Yes, of course." The woman chuckled. "Sorry about that. This is Gigi. I saw your name flash on the screen and didn't realize it was Sebastian's phone. I just assumed you were calling for me. I'm sorry about that."

"Hey, Gigi," Iris said, taking a seat on her couch. She blew out a breath and closed her eyes. "I just needed to ask Sebastian something. Is he available?"

"It'll be a few minutes. He's in the shower. I can have him call you back, or I can keep you on the phone for a minute and we can plan a time to work on your earth magic education. What do you say?"

"That sounds great but..." How did she tell the woman who'd been nothing but kind to her that she just didn't have the energy to think about this right now? She didn't want to push Gigi away, but she also just didn't care about trying more magic at the moment.

"You're on overload, aren't you?" Gigi said, sounding sympathetic. "It's all right. Sebastian told me what you came home to tonight. We can talk about this another time when things aren't so overwhelming."

Relief swept through Iris. "Thanks. I really do want to spend time understanding what I can and can't do, but right now, my anxiety is way too high to focus on anything other than this curse and how to clear my name."

"Understandable. I can't believe this is happening. You do know we're all here for you, right?" Gigi said.

Iris had thought so, but it felt really good to hear the words. After she'd been arrested, she hadn't been able to stop wondering if anyone would believe her innocence. It was irrational since Gigi had sent Sebastian right away to help her. She needed to get a grip. "Thanks for that. I know you mean it. I just... ugh. I'm having trouble trusting anything at the moment. After Sebastian left, I searched my entire house for recording devices just to make sure I'm not being watched. Is that crazy?"

Gigi was silent for a moment before she said, "No. It's not crazy at all. It's completely understandable after the trumped-up charges against you. Who knows what else they're capable of?"

"That's exactly what I keep thinking," Iris admitted. "In fact, that's why I was calling Sebastian. I was hoping he knew someone who could sweep the house for bugs and cameras. I won't feel safe here until I'm sure I'm not being watched."

"Wow. I'm not sure I would've thought of that. Hold on. Here he is."

The phone was passed to Sebastian, who agreed it was a good idea to do a professional sweep of her house. He promised to find someone who was available the next day.

"Fine. I'll drop a key with you because I'll be out for a while in the morning," she said.

After they'd made the arrangements, Iris ended the call and then curled up against the end of her couch, feeling lonelier than ever. She hated that feeling and immediately rose, heading for her spare room where she kept a home gym.

Running on the treadmill usually helped ease her restlessness, but tonight was something else entirely. No matter how fast or hard she ran on her machine, the anger just kept building inside of her until she let out a bloodcurdling scream. And then she just felt empty.

Leaning against the wall, she felt her knees start to buckle, and she let herself slide to the floor where she cried, really cried, for the first time in years. It didn't take long for the sobs to rack her body. She knew it was well past time she let all of her emotions spill out; she hadn't even let herself come undone when she'd ended her marriage. So she held onto her knees and let it all out. By the time her body stopped shaking and her eyes were out of tears, she was spent, exhausted, and ready to curl up in her bed. But before she could make her way into the other room, her doorbell rang.

Iris glanced at the clock. It was just before midnight. Who could be at her door? Kade maybe? He was the only one she could imagine would be knocking on her door that late. She hastily swiped at her eyes, knowing she must look a wreck. She considered running to splash her face with water, but the bell rang again, propelling her to her front door.

"Listen," she started as she swung the door open, but she stopped when she spotted Gigi on her doorstep, holding a bakery box and a thermos. She was wearing a pair of pink flannel pajamas and had matching fluffy slippers on her feet. "Gigi? What are you doing here, sleepwalking?"

"I'm here with reinforcements." She swept into Iris's house. Once she was inside, she held up the thermos and said, "This is Irish coffee and these"—she lifted the box—"are double chocolate fudge cupcakes. I'm here for a slumber party, so where's the bedroom?"

"Bedroom?" Iris asked, stunned.

"Yeah. Bedroom. You don't think we're sleeping on the living room floor like a couple of twelve-year-olds, do you?" She smirked. "This old body won't thank me for that."

Iris couldn't help but chuckle. "Mine either. It's the room at the end of the hall."

"Excellent. Now let's drown our sorrows and resign ourselves to the extra pounds these cupcakes will bring. Ready?"

Iris nodded.

"Good. Follow me." Gigi walked down the hall with purpose as if she owned the place. When she got to the bedroom door, she jerked her head. "Come on and cuddle up with me before I decide these cupcakes are too good to share."

That got Iris moving. She hurried after Gigi and quickly changed into a pair of full-length pajama pants and an old faded T-shirt. Gigi was just climbing onto her bed when Iris grinned at her before taking off and lunging for the Irish coffee.

Gigi shook her head. "I should've known. It's always the stoic, quiet ones who are beasts in bed." Gigi winked at Iris and handed her a cupcake. "Your night is about to get a hundred times better."

"You sure about that?" Iris asked. But then her eyes rolled to the back of her head the moment the cupcake hit her tastebuds. "Never mind," she finally forced out. "You're right. Whoever made these deserves a Nobel Peace Prize for this genius-level masterpiece."

"No argument here," Gigi agreed as she stuffed a pillow between her back and the headboard. The smile on Gigi's face was wide and full of anticipation. "Ready for girl time?"

"What does that mean?" Iris asked, suddenly feeling

skeptical about the visit. Was Gigi really there for girl time, or was she gathering intel? *Dammit, Iris. Paranoid much?*

"It means, Iris Hartsen, that we are going to gorge ourselves on booze and cupcakes and talk about everything and nothing for the next few hours until you pass out."

The sincerity in Gigi's tone, combined with the playful glint in her eye, convinced iris that her new friend was nothing but one hundred percent genuine. She let out a relieved sigh and said, "That sounds just about perfect."

For the next few hours, Iris's attention stayed focused on Gigi as she told funny story after funny story of the mistakes she'd made with her potions and skincare line over the years. Her favorite was when she accidentally used the wrong herb and ended up making Joy a face moisturizer that had caused an allergic reaction and made her lips swell up. Joy had been scheduled for a commercial and had been terrified she'd get fired, but when she walked in to inform the director, he'd praised her for her lip injections and hired her to do three more commercials on the spot. It meant that Gigi needed to recreate the mistake, just so Joy wouldn't get fired.

"You just have no idea how big her lips were, Iris," Gigi said through tears of laughter. "I can't wait for those commercials to come out. I will never not laugh at how that all happened. And for the record, I think her director is blind, because those lips did not fit Joy. She looked like she'd puckered up and kissed a poison ivy plant or something. Not at all sexy, but that's Hollywood for you I guess."

The two women giggled late into the night and by the time Iris finally did pass out, her heart was lighter. And even though she was still worried she might end up in jail for something she didn't do, at least she'd gained a real friend who hopefully would be around for a long time.

CHAPTER SIX

*I*ris was pouring her emergency instant coffee into a travel mug when the doorbell rang.

"I've got it," Gigi called.

"Wait!" Iris called back, not sure why she'd just gone into a mild panic about Gigi finding Kade on the other side of the door. She hurried out of the kitchen and into her living room to find Kade and Gigi introducing themselves.

"We had a sleepover," Gigi said, smiling at Kade. "We were up way too late, downing the sugar and the booze. It's amazing we're both even up this early."

Kade raised one eyebrow. "There was booze, and no one invited me?"

Gigi laughed. "Sorry. Girls' night. You know how it is." Gigi glanced over her shoulder at Iris. "I'm gonna take off and let you get to… whatever it is you two are up to today." There was a hint of suggestion in her tone as she winked at Iris. "Have fun! And remember to be safe. What's that saying? No glove, no love?"

"Oh my god. You have no idea what you're talking about,"

Iris said, laughing as she pressed her spare key into Gigi's hand. "Go home and give this to Sebastian. Your job here is done." She gave her friend a quick hug and whispered, "Thank you for last night. It was exactly what I needed."

"You're welcome." Gigi released her, waved at Kade, and strode out, her blond hair flying behind her.

"She's... fun," Kade said.

"She is now," Iris said, recalling that until very recently, Gigi had been fairly quiet and reserved. But ever since she'd finally learned the truth about her mother's disappearance, she'd found closure and seemed genuinely happy with Sebastian and her friendship with the other coven members. Iris was pleased for her and wished she was as content with her own life. "When she first got to Premonition Pointe a little over a year ago, she mostly kept to herself. Now that she's made friends and has a new relationship, she's really come out of her shell."

"Sounds like she's found her place," Kade said.

Iris nodded. "I think so."

"Just like you," he said with a soft smile. "If you don't mind me asking, what's with Sebastian? He's your lawyer, right?"

She nodded.

"Are they together? I overheard you asking her to give him your key."

"He's her boyfriend. He's going to get someone to sweep my place for any surveillance. I know that sounds paranoid, but..." She lifted her hands palms up and shrugged. "Better safe than sorry, right?"

"After everything that happened yesterday, I'd say it's just smart." He smiled at her. "Ready to go learn Tad's secrets?"

"More than ready." Iris grabbed her travel mug of coffee and followed Kade out to his gray Honda CR-V. "I think this might be the perfect car for following someone."

"Why's that?" he asked as he held the door open for her.

"It just looks like every other small SUV on the road."

"Ouch," he said playfully. "Are you calling me basic?"

"If the SUV fits," she teased and climbed into the car.

He chuckled and shook his head as he jogged around to the other side and hopped into the driver's seat. "You're feisty this morning. I like it."

"It's probably all the sugar I ate last night," she said and took a long sip of her coffee.

He glanced over at her. "I was going to stop for some coffee at the café, but it looks like you're a step ahead of me."

Iris's eyebrows shot up. "You're still pre-coffee?"

"Yep."

"And you're this awake? Good god, man. How do you do it?" she asked, horrified. Without at least two cups of coffee in the morning, Iris couldn't even manage to tie her shoelaces, let alone hold a conversation.

"Good genes." He grinned and pulled into the drive-thru of their neighborhood coffee shop. Five minutes later, with a large latte and a slice of coffee cake, he sped north, away from town toward the exclusive cliffside neighborhood where Tad lived.

It hadn't been difficult for Iris to find his address. She still had the passwords to the city databases. Five minutes on the tax assessor's site and she had everything she needed. Obviously, no one had thought to change any of the logins since they'd ousted her. It was careless on their part, but good luck for her.

On the first pass, Kade rolled by Tad's house, giving Iris a chance to check it out. His flashy silver Ferrari sat in the driveway of a three-story house that looked over the dramatic coastline.

"Whoa. Looks like someone is living the life," Iris said, unable to imagine having the kind of money to live in such a home on the California coast.

"It's the only kind of life he knows," Kade said, turning around at the end of a cul-de-sac. "Privileged doesn't begin to cover it."

"I sense some resentment there." Iris studied him, taking in his casual attire of jeans, a T-shirt, and well-worn sneakers, though she noticed they were a quality brand. "You grew up in his world. Weren't you given the same privilege?"

He let out a huff of humorless laughter. "Hardly. We went to the same boarding school, but I was the scholarship kid. He was the kid who had an entire building named after him because his parents donated a bunch of money to get him out of trouble."

"No way. That didn't really happen, did it?"

"Yep. It really did." He parked the SUV a half block away from Tad's house and let the engine idle. "He's never had to work for anything. Or at least he didn't back then. Doesn't seem like it now either, since some powerful friends appointed him to your position."

Iris ground her teeth together. It still stung that a man with no service or municipal leadership experience had been handed the keys to Premonition Pointe. "You seem to not like him very much. Is this personal for you?"

"No. Not at all." Kade shrugged. "To be honest, I haven't really thought about him at all until after I moved here and learned he'd been appointed the new mayor a few days ago. So I'm just stating facts."

"I appreciate that." Iris sipped more of her coffee, keeping her eyes trained on Tad's front door. "Do you think we're wasting our time?"

"What do you mean?" he asked.

"What if he just goes straight to work?" Iris glanced at Kade. "If that happens, all we'll learn is whether or not he's adept at adhering to traffic laws."

"It's possible he'll go straight there, but I doubt it. I've seen him running around town most mornings."

"You have?" she asked, intrigued. "What are you doing up and around town in the mornings?"

He smirked at her. "Wouldn't you like to know?"

"Yes. Yes, I would." She narrowed her eyes at him. "Why so secretive?" Then it occurred to her that maybe she was getting a little too personal. If he was out early in the morning, maybe that meant he hadn't actually ever gone home.

"What's that look?" he asked with an amused glance.

"Nothing. I... You don't have to answer."

He barked out a laugh. "You're thinking I'm out doing the walk of shame, aren't you?"

Her face heated. "Sorry. Whatever, or *whoever* you're doing, it's none of my business."

Kade's bright blue eyes danced with amusement. "You're pretty adorable when you're flustered."

"I'm not adorable," Iris insisted. "Adorable is for twenty-year-olds, not a woman who is just shy of fifty."

"I disagree." He reached over and tucked a lock of her hair behind her ear. "I have only known you for twenty-four hours, but it's obvious you're a smart woman with one hell of a backbone. And seeing you a little bit flustered and blushing *is* adorable. I feel like you don't let your guard down a lot. I like that I get a glimpse of that side of you."

Iris's cheeks heated again, and she couldn't believe that at her age she could still get flustered because a gorgeous man was being nice to her.

"There it is again." He pressed his palm to her warm cheek. "I like it."

"I don't," she lied even as she leaned into his palm. How long had it been since someone had touched her so tenderly? Even though she hadn't been divorced that long, Tom hadn't shown her that sort of affection in years.

"Yes, you do." He brushed his thumb over her cheek before dropping his hand. Kade started to say something else, but Iris cut him off as she pointed at Tad's house.

"Tad's headed for his car." She leaned forward, peering out the window at the overly slick man. Even from their vantage point a half block away, she could see he'd overused the gel again.

"Ready for some sleuthing?" he asked, putting the Honda into gear.

"I've been ready," she said, pulling out her phone, wanting to be prepared if she needed to take any pictures.

"I bet." As Tad sped down the street, Kade eased out of the spot and followed, keeping a decent distance between them so that they wouldn't be spotted.

Tad stopped at the same café where Kade had gotten his coffee that morning, and Iris decided he wasn't a total psycho. However, stopping at a café wasn't going to help them dig up his secrets. She felt the same way when he went through the drive through pharmacy and then dropped a package off at the post office.

"I think this stakeout was a bust," Iris said when Tad finally pulled into the mayor's parking spot in front of the administrative offices.

"Most likely. But we could try again tomorrow if you want," Kade said, coming to a stop at the red light just past city hall.

Iris glanced over and sucked in a sharp breath when she

spotted a younger woman in a Magical Task Force uniform leaning against the building with a phone pressed to her ear. "Looks like an investigator has been sent in."

Kade followed her gaze. "Just one? Doesn't seem like they are taking the curse that seriously then."

"I honestly didn't think they'd send anyone." Iris didn't know what to make of the development. On the one hand, the MTF was well known for their professionalism and had a high standard for investigating cases. On the other, this one looked fresh out of training camp, and who knew what kind of influence Tad and the town council might exert over her. They'd likely expect her to just do whatever it took to find someone responsible and close the books on it as quickly as possible.

"What do you think it means then?" he asked, eyeing the younger woman. "Are they really worried about the state of things in Premonition Pointe, or is it something else?"

"My gut says something else, but I don't know what that would be," Iris said, slumping back into her seat.

"We could talk to her and see if she reveals anything," Kade said, already pulling his car into a parking space near the park.

"We could, but I doubt it would work yet. She's too fresh on the assignment. Let's give her a day or so to settle in, and then we'll randomly run into her and just start making friendly conversation. Most people love talking about themselves, so we'll start there."

Kade studied her for a moment. "You seem more like a former investigator than a former mayor right now. Are you just a natural at this?"

She chuckled. "You'd be surprised at how often the jobs overlapped in the last few years. I found myself spending a lot of time with the DA and the assistant DA, trying to eradicate the crime that keeps trying to creep into this town. It wasn't the most enjoyable aspect of the job, but it was necessary."

"No doubt." Kade climbed out of the SUV and went around to open her door. "I think it's time for breakfast."

Iris glanced at her watch, mindful that he had a job to get to that day. But there was plenty of time to get something to eat, and besides, she wanted nothing more than to support the business owners of the town. With the tourists missing in action, the businesses really needed local support more than ever.

CHAPTER SEVEN

*I*ris led Kade a few blocks over to Blueberries, a farm-to-table restaurant that was one of Iris's favorites. The woman who owned it lived just a few miles inland on a farm where they grew most of the ingredients.

"I hope this is okay," Iris said as they walked inside. As suspected, the restaurant was mostly empty, but a few locals were sitting at the bar drinking Bloody Marys.

"It looks great," Kade agreed.

"Wait until you try the ricotta blueberry pancakes. You'll die a happy man." Iris waved to Mandy, the owner, who'd spotted them and was rushing over. She was an older woman with gorgeous, long silver hair and a bright, welcoming smile.

"Iris!" the woman cried and swept her into her arms. "I'm so glad you're here. I've been worried about you ever since I heard the news."

"It's just a job. I'll figure something out," Iris said, assuming she was referring to the mayor's position.

The woman pulled back and frowned. "I meant about the arrest yesterday. The entire town is talking about it. I can't believe they really think you're the one who cast the curse. Anyone with half a brain already knows that casting spells isn't in your wheelhouse."

While Iris appreciated the support, it frustrated her that Mandy didn't believe that she cast the curse because of her abilities instead of the fact that Iris loved Premonition Pointe and would never do anything to hurt the residents. Shouldn't Mandy know that about her?

"Iris?" Mandy asked. "Are you all right?"

"Yes, of course," she said automatically. "And thanks for the support. It is pretty crazy, right?"

Mandy placed a hand on Iris's arm and squeezed gently. "They'll figure it out soon enough, and then they'll have to apologize for jumping to conclusions."

"I'm not counting on an apology," Iris said. "I just want them to find out who really did this before they do something worse."

Kade moved closer and placed his hand on the small of her back. "If they don't, we will."

"Good man," Mandy said, eyeing him with appreciation. She held her hand out to him. "We haven't met. I'm Mandy, owner of this little café. And you are?"

"Kade Carson." He shook her hand. "I'm Iris's new neighbor."

"Well, isn't that lucky." She pumped her eyebrows at Iris. "He's a major step up from that disappointing ex of yours."

Iris chuckled. "I agree, but don't get too excited. Kade's just a friend."

Mandy eyed him again and then looked back at Iris. "Yeah, just keep telling yourself that." She winked at them. "Let me get you a table before I starve you to death." Mandy led them to a table by the window and left them with a couple of menus.

Iris watched her go and then turned her attention to Kade. "Sorry about that. I don't know why she just assumed we are a thing."

"It's all right. I don't mind if people think I'm dating my gorgeous neighbor." He gave her a sexy half smile and turned his attention to the menu.

"Oh, really?" She let out a surprised laugh, completely taken off guard by his flirting.

"Yep. In fact, I wouldn't mind if it was true."

Iris blinked at him. "What?" He wasn't serious, was he? They'd just met, and she was under criminal investigation. "Are you crazy?"

"No." He held her gaze as he asked, "Why is that crazy?"

"Because of my drama. There are charges against me for cursing the town, remember?"

"Sure, but since I'm your alibi, I already know you didn't do it. So I'm confident those charges won't hold up." He glanced up as Mandy approached with water.

"Have you decided what you're having today?"

"Iris says I need the ricotta blueberry pancakes, so that's what I'm having," Kade said. "With a side of thick bacon and a very large cup of coffee."

Iris ordered the same, and when Mandy returned to the kitchen, she said, "You can't possibly want to date someone after only knowing them for two days."

"Date, as in a reoccurring thing, is premature, but I would like to take you out on *a date*. Dinner? Maybe a daytime hike or a bike ride along the coastal trail? What do you say?"

"A date?" she parroted like a fool. It had been a very long time since anyone had asked her out, and even longer since they'd proposed something she'd really like to do.

Kade just gave her that sexy smile again and then took a sip of his water.

"When?" she asked.

"This weekend? Saturday morning? How about a sunrise hike?"

There was no turning down an offer like that. If she were to describe her perfect date, that would be it. "Yes. I'd love to."

His face lit up with a smile. "You won't regret it."

"I'm sure I won't."

When their meals arrived, Iris waited for Kade to take his first bite and was rewarded with his satisfied moan of pleasure.

"Sweet hell fire, these are incredible," he said, shoving another forkful into his mouth.

"Just think of all the other meals I can introduce you to in this town," Iris said, taking a bite of her own pancakes.

"You know that thing I said about it being too soon to be dating?" he said.

"Yeah?"

"I take it back. We're officially dating now. No backing out until you've introduced me to all the culinary wonders of this town."

Iris laughed. "When you put it that way… I'm in. We'll eat our way through town until we've each gained thirty pounds."

"Couples that gain together, stay together," he teased.

Damn, he was adorable. Iris wanted to lean across the table and kiss him right there in Blueberries. If they'd already been on a date or two, she would have, but instead, she focused on her pancakes and smiled to herself. Yesterday she'd had the worst day in memory, and now she was sitting across from a man who not only made her smile, he also made her heart race. They weren't on a date, but it sure felt like it.

"There you are!" an all too familiar and unwelcome voice called across the restaurant.

Iris jerked her head up and blinked, praying that she was seeing and hearing things.

"Iris!" Katheryn West was wearing a perfectly tailored black suit with a lavender silk blouse and her prized Louboutin heels. Her hair was about three shades blonder than the last time Iris had seen her, and her fake tan was about two shades darker. She swept past Mandy and strode over to their table. Without saying a word, she dragged Iris out of her chair, pulling her into a tight hug.

Iris stiffened and didn't hug her mother back. "Mom, what are you doing here?"

"I came as soon as I heard." She pulled back and ran her hands over Iris's face as if checking for abnormalities.

Iris jerked away. "What are you doing?"

"I'm just making sure no one touched you while you were locked up in prison." She scanned Iris's arms and turned her around as if she could see through her clothes.

"I wasn't in prison, Mother," Iris said, turning back around and crossing her arms over her chest in a defensive stance. "My lawyer got me released right after the charges were filed. There's nothing to be worried about."

"Nothing to be worried about? My baby finally found her magic and ended up cursing an entire town. This is all my fault that I couldn't manage to teach you to control your powers. It's up to me to fix it." Katheryn sank dramatically into one of the empty chairs and rested her wrist against her forehead.

"Oh my god," Iris muttered. "You can't be serious."

Her mother dropped her hand and gaped at her daughter. "I'm as serious as the tax man. If I'd done my job better, you wouldn't be in this position. I've called my lawyer. He's the best in the business, so we'll do everything we can to either get the charges dropped or get you a reduced sentence. Then we'll get you classes so you can control that magic of yours and maybe some therapy to control your repressed anger. No one casts a curse like that without having unresolved issues."

A spike of fury rushed through Iris's veins. "Mother, back off. I have a lawyer. I'm sorry you came all this way, but your help isn't needed."

Katheryn tsked. "Don't be stubborn, baby. I know it's overwhelming, but if we just make a plan, we—"

"Mother, stop!" Iris stood. "You can't just come here with all kinds of wrong assumptions and try to take over. It doesn't work that way."

"Iris, I'm only trying to help," she said, her eyes sad and full of disappointment.

Kade cleared his throat, making them both turn to him.

"Well, who is this?" Katheryn asked with judgment lacing her tone. "New boyfriend? Did he have anything to do with your outburst that put a curse on this town?"

Iris groaned while Kade choked on a piece of bacon. "I'm sorry," Iris said to Kade. Then she turned to her mother. "You need to leave."

"I'm not going anywhere. I'm here to help!"

"Um, Mrs.—" Kade started.

"It's Ms. West. Katheryn West. And you are?" She swept her gaze over him, not doing a thing to hide her judgment.

"I'm Kade Carson, Iris's neighbor." He held his hand out. "It's nice to meet you."

Katheryn pursed her lips together and reluctantly shook his hand. "Are you saying you're not dating my daughter?"

Kade raised one eyebrow. "I didn't say anything. But I'm not sure that it's any of your business if we're dating or not."

Iris wanted to cheer at his response. There was nothing sexier than someone standing up to her overbearing mother.

"By the way," Kade added. "Your daughter didn't cast that curse." He stood, threw some money down on the table and said, "Iris, I have to get to work. Do you need a ride home?"

"I have a car. She'll be fine," Katheryn said, grabbing Iris's wrist as if she were going to force her to stay by her side.

Iris wrenched her arm out of her mother's grip. She desperately wanted to take him up on his offer but knew she just needed to stay and deal with her mother. If Iris didn't get her to see reason, she'd just make more plans for Iris's life that she had no intention of following through on. "I can manage. Go on. Tell Lucas I said hello."

Kade glanced at Katheryn and then back at Iris. "Are you sure?"

She nodded. "Thanks again."

He smiled. "I'm looking forward to Saturday."

"Me, too." She couldn't help the smile that claimed her lips as he walked away, even though she immediately regretted it when she saw the scowl on her mother's face. Iris sighed. "Seriously, Mother. Why are you here? You do realize that I'm a grown woman who is more than capable of handling my own life, right?"

"That seems dubious, considering you cursed the town you claim to love. Though I admit I don't quite understand the appeal." She tapped her fingernails on the table. "Why don't you come home with me while we let this situation cool down a bit. Let my lawyers—"

"Do you never listen to me?" Iris demanded. "I didn't curse the town, and I have both a lawyer and an alibi. Sebastian is dealing with it. I don't need you to swoop in here and try to take over."

"Iris, you need some perspective. Charges like this don't just go away. Now let me do what I do, and all of this will be over before you know it."

Iris rolled her eyes, added some money to the pile Kade had left on the table, and then turned and walked out. She was not going to stand there any longer and let her mother treat her like a petulant teenager.

Of course, Katheryn followed her. "You're being stubborn again," she said once they were out on the sidewalk.

"Fine. I'm stubborn. I'm okay with that," Iris said. "At least we know I got one trait from you."

"Stop being flippant." Katheryn fell into step beside Iris. "This is serious."

"You're damned right it's serious," a man said from behind them.

Iris spun around to see Tad standing there, practically snarling at her.

"How dare you do this to me," he hissed, glaring at Iris. "Just because you were ousted, that doesn't give you the right to mess with the livelihoods of every person who lives and works in this town."

"I didn't curse Premonition Pointe. Everyone who's known me for longer than five minutes knows that about me," Iris said as evenly as she could, aware that her own mother seemed to have no problem believing the worst about her. She put that thought out of her mind and continued, "If I were you, I'd start really looking in another direction if you want to figure out who did this."

"You're the only one with a motive, Hartsen. Even your husband thinks you did it," Tad spat and straightened his bright yellow tie.

"Ex-husband," Iris clarified. "And if he had any brains left at all, even he'd realize how absurd that accusation is."

"I'm on to you, Hartsen. Mark my words. By the time the DA is done with the investigation, you'll be behind bars for so long you'll be ninety before you see freedom again."

Katheryn took a step forward, invading Tad's personal space as she stared him down, wrinkling her nose at him. "You're a sad, pathetic little man. Don't you have anything better to do than yell at Iris? Like go figure out how to reverse this curse before all the residents leave for greener pastures?" She turned to Iris. "Who hired this idiot?"

Iris couldn't help the laugh that flew out of her mouth at her mother's unexpected insult.

"I was appointed by the town council," Tad said. "They had to do something before the town was completely run into the ground by her." He nodded at Iris. "The drug stats went up by fifty percent during her tenure. Did you know that?"

"Only because we were doing something to stop the drug trafficking. The administration before me turned a blind eye and refused to acknowledge there was even a problem. If it doesn't exist, there aren't any stats."

Tad sputtered as he tried to come up with some way to contradict her explanation, but his face just turned red as he said, "Go to hell. Both of you."

Iris just shrugged as he strode into Blueberries, his limbs jerky with anger.

"Come on, Iris. Let's get home. I want to unpack before we really dig into your case," Katheryn said.

It was on the tip of Iris's tongue to once again tell her mother to mind her own business, but she stopped herself, remembering she'd had her back with Tad. That one moment when her mother had told him off had made all the rest of the harassment worth it. Besides, she knew from experience there was no stopping her mom until she laid out every detail of her plan whether Iris wanted to hear it or not.

"All right, but I'm driving," Iris said, holding out her hand for the keys to her mother's BMW.

"Iris, you know I don't let other people drive," Katheryn said. "Just get in and I'll take you home."

"Nope. Not this time." Iris gestured for the keys and stood there until her mother finally caved and handed them over. Iris hid her smile as she slid in behind the wheel. Once her mother was in the passenger seat, Iris laid into the gas and enjoyed every minute of driving her mother's luxury car, knowing that moment was likely the last pleasurable one they'd share until her mother's unexpected visit finally came to an end.

CHAPTER EIGHT

"*W*hy are there people here?" Katheryn asked, peering out the windshield of her BMW. "And a work van? Iris, what is going on?"

Iris gritted her teeth. "It's just my lawyer and a technical team, making sure my house is safe after everything that happened." She sure as hell wasn't going to tell her mother she was having the place swept for surveillance. Who knew what she'd think of that?

"What kind of technical team?" she asked, her eyes narrowed. Katheryn could be intentionally obtuse sometimes, but she wasn't stupid.

Iris shrugged and climbed out, hoping to avoid the conversation until later.

The passenger door slammed so hard it made Iris jump. She glanced over to find her mother striding toward the house, determination etched on her face. As soon as she opened the door, she raised her voice and demanded to speak to whoever was in charge.

Sebastian appeared from the side of the house, frowning.

When he spotted Iris, he strode over. "Who's that?"

"My mother." She sucked in a cleansing breath. "I'll apologize in advance. Her way of 'helping' is to take over and push everyone around."

He winced. "Sounds painful."

"It is. Which is why I'm asking you now that if it's at all possible, don't mention you were sweeping my house for surveillance. I really don't want to know what she'd do if she thought anyone had planted a teddy cam somewhere."

"You got it," he said with a nod. "But you should probably know that we did find a couple of cameras in your house."

Iris's entire body went cold. She'd known it was a possibility. Why else would she search her house and then called Sebastian for professionals? But deep down, she'd thought she was being paranoid.

"One was in your living room and the other in your kitchen, so at least they weren't watching your bedroom or worse," Sebastian continued.

"Thank the gods for small favors," she whispered. Her stomach churned, and she prayed she didn't vomit right there in her front yard.

"My guys are putting in a security system, so we'll know if anyone tries to get inside to replant the cameras. I hope that's okay. I called, but when I didn't hear back from you, I made a decision."

"Of course, it's fine." She turned to him, giving him a grateful smile. "I appreciate that."

"There's more," he said, his tone grave.

Iris closed her eyes for a moment. "Okay, hit me."

"The cameras have been there longer than twenty-four hours."

"What?" Iris's eyes were wide now as she stared at him in

horror. "How long have I been being watched?" And why? But she didn't ask him that. How could he possibly know?

"We think for at least three months." He stared at the front of the house where Katheryn was interrogating one of the workers. "Do you think Tom put them in to see if he could get something to use in the divorce?"

A sharp stab of pain pierced Iris's heart. She pressed her hand to her chest and tried to breathe. Because if it was three months ago, he was probably right. And even though she was done with Tom, she'd still spent years of her life with the man. She'd trusted him at one time. Those days were long over after everything he'd put her through over the last year. Her stomach rolled at the thought of him bugging her house. She didn't want to believe it, but who else would've done it? Someone from the council who was trying to get dirt to oust her? She couldn't imagine that. Besides, Tom was the one with access. Finally, she nodded and said, "That makes the most sense."

"Are you sure it's a good idea to have all these people milling around your house?" Katheryn asked as she approached them, though her tone was softer, and the aggression had vanished.

"They're putting in an alarm, Mom. What's wrong with that?" Iris asked, pressing her fingers to her temples to try to relieve the sudden headache.

"Nothing. It just seems like a lot of strangers, that's all." She peered at Sebastian. "Who are you?"

"Sebastian Knight. I'm Iris's lawyer and the one who arranged the team to secure her home." He held his hand out to her.

She straightened her shoulders and then shook his hand reluctantly. "I'm sure you're a fine lawyer Sebastian, but your services are no longer needed. My lawyer will take things from here."

"Mother!" Iris snapped. "What do you think you're doing?" She turned to Sebastian, who was rocked back on his heels with his hands in his pockets. "That's not true. I'm not firing you, and I'm not hiring her lawyer. Please ignore everything she just said."

"Iris!" Katheryn hissed. She yanked on Iris's arm and pulled her a few feet away from Sebastian. "Lester is the best in the business. You can't just say no. What if you end up in jail because you were too proud to accept my help? When will you stop being so self-destructive?"

Iris blinked at her, still trying to process what she'd said. Then when it sank in, she scoffed and let all of her frustrations fly. "*I'm* self-destructive? You've got to be kidding me. What about you, Mom? Five different husbands in eight years? Two bankrupted businesses? And a feud with your best friend because she wanted to move to another state to be near her daughter? Who exactly is the self-destructive one?"

Katheryn went white with shock, no doubt because Iris had never called her out on her bullshit before. But she'd gone too far this time. Iris turned to Sebastian, her face hot with embarrassment. The last thing she'd wanted to do was air her family's dirty laundry in front of other people, especially him. He was Gigi's boyfriend, and she'd just started a friendship with her. "I'm really sorry about this. I swear, I never have this much drama."

He nodded and gave her a sympathetic smile. "Trust me, I've seen my fair share of drama, and while this is pretty serious, you're not the one causing it. It's okay. I'll give you guys a few minutes, and when you're done, I'll make sure you know how to use the alarm, all right?"

Iris wanted to hug him. Instead, she nodded and turned to her mother, who had crouched down and was breathing heavily and dramatically pressing her palm to her chest.

"I can't… believe… you said that," she wheezed.

Iris struggled to keep from rolling her eyes. Talk about drama. "We'll talk about it later. Just try to calm down, okay?"

Katheryn eyed her daughter, irritation flashing in her blue eyes.

Yeah, she was fine. Iris knew she was just biding her time until she could lay into her again. "It looks like the guys are finishing up. Why don't you wait here while they show me how to use this new security system?"

Her mother didn't respond. She just turned her head and stared down the tree-lined street.

Shaking her head, Iris caught up with Sebastian, tried to pay attention while he showed her how to use the new house alarm, and then thanked him as he and the technicians left.

"We'll try to see if we can trace the cameras back to anyone. Fingerprints, DNA or tracking the serial numbers," he said.

"Is that likely?" she asked, imagining that it couldn't be that easy.

"No. But it won't stop us from looking." He gave her a tiny smile. "No stone unturned."

"Right." She was watching her mother, who was talking and laughing with one of the techs. All signs of her meltdown were gone as she smiled up at him and patted his chest with her hand.

"You've got your hands full there," Sebastian said.

"You don't know the half of it," she said with a sigh. "If I can just convince her that the case is under control, I might be able to get her to go home. But it's not looking good."

"I'd guess you're right."

They both watched as Katheryn made one of the techs walk her through everything they'd done that day.

Iris patted Sebastian on the arm. "Thanks for everything you've done today. Do I need to write someone a check?"

"Nah. It's covered."

"What do you mean, it's covered?" Iris asked, frowning at him.

He just shrugged and called out to the crew. "Time to go, guys. Our work here is done."

"Sebastian?" Iris asked, waiting for an answer.

He smiled, waved, and strode toward his car. A few moments later, Iris was left with just her mother. She pulled out her phone and sent a text to Gigi, asking why Sebastian wouldn't accept any payment.

Gigi: *Because I told him I was covering it.*

Iris texted back. *Why?*

Because I can.

Gigi! I can't accept that.

The green dots flashed for entirely too long before the next text came through. *Okay, but can we talk about it first?*

Iris pressed Gigi's number, and when she answered, Iris said, "Okay, let's talk."

"You're quick," Gigi said. "I'd rather do this in person. Can you get away? Maybe stop by here? I'd like to show you something."

Iris stared at her house. Her mother had disappeared inside, and Iris couldn't resist the excuse to give them some time apart so that they each could cool down a bit before they had the inevitable discussion that Iris had been avoiding for the past thirty-five years. "Sure. Text me your address and then give me a few minutes."

"I'll be here," Gigi said happily. "And Iris?"

"Yeah?"

"Remember that none of this is your fault, and you didn't do anything to deserve all the shitty things happening right now."

The words were like a gut punch, because that was exactly how she was starting to feel. She opened her mouth to thank Gigi, but nothing came out. After clearing her throat, she finally forced out a barely audible thanks and then ended the call.

"Iris, get in here!" Katheryn called. "With your luck, someone is likely to run you down right there on your own lawn."

She probably wasn't wrong. Iris walked up to the house and stood in the doorway. "I need to run out for a while."

"What?" Katheryn balked. When she spoke again, it was in her mom voice. "But I just got here, and we have things to talk about."

Iris bristled at her mother's tone, but she forced herself to not react. "I'm sorry about that, but I do have somewhere I have to be. And I think we can both use a little time to cool off."

"I don't need—"

"Bye, Mom." Iris closed the door and made a beeline for her car. She was pulling out of the driveway when she spotted her mother tugging the front door open. Iris waved as she sped by and then let out a huge sigh of relief. The ache in her gut disappeared, an even her headache started to fade. Ever since her mother had walked into Blueberries, she'd been wound so tight that it was a miracle she hadn't had a full-blown panic attack. Feeling better, Iris lowered the window and turned up the radio, enjoying the solitary drive to Gigi's house.

CHAPTER NINE

*W*hen Iris pulled into Gigi's driveway, she got out of the car and took a moment to study the gorgeous Victorian seaside home. Her skin tingled, feeling suspiciously like magic. Everything about the house called to her and without conscious thought, she started to move up the cobblestone path toward the foliage-covered gate that led to the front door.

The closer she got to the house, the stronger the magic got, making her almost vibrate with it. The only other time she'd felt magic like that had been the day before when the curse had been cast over Premonition Pointe and afterwards while she was at the cliff with the coven. But this felt different. Better. Intoxicating. She thought she should be more apprehensive about the unknown, but she wasn't. She just wanted more.

Just before she got to Gigi's door, it swung open and a strong breeze came from behind her, almost pushing her into the house.

"Uh, Gigi," she called as she stepped through the threshold.

"I really hope this is your house or else I could be making a huge mistake."

She heard her new friend's laugh before she spotted her near the stairs in another one of her flowy skirts and peasant blouses. This time she was barefooted, and her hair was twisted up into a bun with a pencil holding it in place.

"This is you just hanging out at home. That's not fair. Am I the only one who looks like a troll without at least an hour of maintenance?"

"Nope. That's me, too," a man's voice rang out as Skyler Cole followed Gigi into the room. He was the owner of Sky's the Limit, a high-end boutique on the town square that carried new and used clothing. "When Pete tells me what time we need to leave, it's usually an hour earlier than we really need to hit the road. He's learned I need a cushion to look this fabulous."

Iris laughed. Skyler was wearing skinny jeans, a fitted T-shirt, and a blazer. But what really caught her attention was his fabulous purple and pink eye-makeup. Iris was certain she'd never managed to look that good even when she was twenty-one and still trying to impress everyone around her. "Hi, Skyler. It's nice to see you again."

Skyler didn't say a word as he walked over to her and engulfed her in a hug. He held on tightly and said, "It's not right what they're doing to you. I can't even believe they think you cast the curse."

Iris was at a loss for words. She knew Skyler of course. Iris knew all the business owners in town. She'd made a point of it, always wanting to know what they needed from the city to be successful. Skyler hadn't really needed her help, but she'd still stopped in when he was getting his shop ready and always listened when he had feedback about the permitting process or parking issues or anything else that was on his mind.

"Thanks," Iris said when he finally let her go. "The support means a lot."

"Of course. I swear, that new mayor, Tad? He's a grade-A douche," Skyler said, his expression full of ire. "Do you know what he did this afternoon?"

Iris shook her head.

"He sent every business in town a bill to pay for the Magical Task Force investigators. One thousand dollars is due by the end of the week, or we'll be shut down."

"He did what?" Iris cried, already pulling out her phone. Her fingers were already dialing before she even knew what she was doing. As the phone rang, she said, "That's not legal. No one can be levied an extra tax without a vote."

"He said it was a 'special assessment,' not a tax," Skyler said.

Iris wanted to scream. "Special assessments have to be voted on by the town council. But there are limits. A thousand dollars within a week is well beyond that boundary."

"That's what I thought," he said. "But when he's walking around with two policemen, most aren't going to question it. No one wants to be the squeaky wheel. They're too busy trying to keep the lights on with no customers."

"Iris? What is it?" Julie asked through the phone.

Holding a finger up, indicating she needed a moment, Iris turned around and paced as she asked, "What do you know about this thousand-dollar assessment the council put into place on all of Premonition Pointe's businesses?"

"What assessment?" Julie asked, sounding genuinely surprised. "A thousand dollars? That's... not right. Where did you hear this?"

Iris turned back around and asked Skyler, "Did Tad leave a written bill or paperwork of some kind?"

Skyler nodded, reached into his back pocket, and produced the bill in question.

"You just happened to have it with you?" Iris asked him.

"I was going to ask Sebastian about it, but apparently he was busy at your place all day." He winked at her, making sure she knew he was only teasing.

"Sorry about that," she said, forcing a smile even as she scanned the bill. Immediately, she knew something was wrong. It wasn't the correct form for an assessment. The taxpayer ID was missing, and there was no way to reference the record at all. The bill looked like a mass mailing, which begged the question of how they were going to log payments or even where those funds were going to be held. "Julie, I have the form. You didn't type this up?"

"Tad gave me the afternoon off after the MTF agent showed up," she said, her tone changing from concerned to frustrated. "He told me there wasn't enough going on to justify paying me."

"That jackass," Iris said.

Julie chuckled. "You know, I think that's the most candid thing I've ever heard you say."

"Well, stick around, cause it's about to get real now," she said. "If Tad sent you home, who else was left in the office? The MTF agent and... anyone else?"

"Not at the mayor's office," Julie said. "When I left, no one else was there. He might have called in one of the interns, I guess. Someone had to type the form, and let me tell you, it wasn't Tad. He can barely turn the computer on, much less format a bill."

"Can you do me a favor and go down the list and see if he did call in anyone?" Iris asked, running a hand through her hair. It was a tic of hers when she was feeling particularly helpless. Without more information, there wasn't a lot she could do about what appeared to be fraud.

"Yeah. I can do that. I'll call you as soon as I know anything."

Iris thanked Julie and then turned to Skyler. "I don't have the answers yet, but it looks suspiciously like this bill is illegal. If I were you, I wouldn't pay it. If my theory is correct, they won't pursue collections on it."

He nodded and held his hand out for the bill.

Iris glanced down at it and then at Gigi. "Do you happen to have a copy machine or a fax that will make copies? I'd really like to keep this so I can compare it to an official assessment or emergency levy, both of which we ordered while I was mayor."

"Of course. Who doesn't have a copier these days?" Gigi grabbed it and told them to follow her as she made her way down the hall to an oversized office.

The magic Iris had felt when she first arrived was back and soothing the anxiety that had started to take over. Her shoulders relaxed, and finally her headache vanished.

"Is your house spelled?" Iris asked Gigi as she fiddled with her copier.

"Spelled? What do you mean?" Gigi glanced over her shoulder, her brows furrowed in confusion.

"I can feel magic in the air, and... I don't know. It feels like you cast a happiness spell or something. It's unlike anything I've felt before. It's soothing, I guess."

Skyler and Gigi shared a glanced before Gigi walked over to them and handed the bill back to Skyler and a copy to Iris. "My house isn't spelled. Or at least not formally."

"What does that mean?" Iris asked. "Not intentionally?"

Gigi smiled and walked to the door. She gestured for them to follow her.

They left the office and entered the room next door. Iris stood in the doorway, her head spinning as magic washed over her. The air was thick with it, and it energized Iris, making her feel like she could do anything. Iris had never been high before, but she imagined it would feel like this room.

"This is... wonderful," Iris said, finally taking a look around and spotting rows and rows of fresh and dried herbs. One wall housed extra inventory of Gigi's skincare line that they sold at Skyler's shop. It was then that she realized the room was where her friend did a lot of her spell casting. Was that why it was so thick with magic? Certainly, but why did her magic linger?

"It's because of the plants," Gigi said quietly. "They soak up the magic and give it off naturally, making any spell room an oasis to the practitioner. Or at least that's how it works for the more powerful earth witches."

Gigi and Iris were both blessed with earth magic, but Gigi had been the only one to explore it. Or master it, as seemed to be the case. Iris, on the other hand, was a newbie in the magic department. Gigi studied Iris, and after a moment, a huge grin broke out over her face. "You're almost drunk on the magic, aren't you?"

Iris nodded. "It was really strong when I first got here, but once I was inside, it sort of faded. Then when we got closer to this room, it came roaring back. I gotta say, you better haul me out of here or else I just might never leave. I don't think I've ever felt this good before."

"Oh boy. The former mayor has found her kryptonite," Skyler said, chuckling. "It's really fun to watch."

"Agreed," Gigi said. "But as great as it is to see her walls crumble, I'd really like to see what she could do here. If she's feeling this good off of residual magic... Well, I suspect she'll be able to give me a run for my money once she knows a few tricks."

"You still want to help me with my earth magic?" Iris asked her, praying that was true. If Gigi asked her to leave right that moment, she would, but it would be painful.

"Absolutely. Today if you have some time," Gigi said with a huge smile.

"Sure," Iris said quickly. But then she sobered as she remembered why she'd come over in the first place. "First, we need to talk about why you think I don't need to be paying Sebastian for my legal expenses."

Gigi waved an impatient hand. "Yeah, yeah. But I want to know if you want to work on beauty products or potions first."

"Potions," Iris said automatically. She'd always wanted to learn to make energy potions or medicinal potions for headaches or allergies. Something someone could drink on the go and get what they needed without a big production.

"All right. That's doable," Gigi said with a nod. "Now, let's get a snack and work out the money issue before we get to work in the herb studio."

Iris cast the room a longing look before reluctantly pulling away and following Gigi and Skyler into the kitchen, where she sat at the bar and waited for Gigi to explain why she was insisting on paying her legal fees.

Iris had been expecting a lecture about letting friends help friends, but what she learned instead blew her mind. By the time Gigi was done explaining, tears were flowing down Iris's cheeks, and she knew that no matter what else happened, she would be friends with Gigi forever. She was just that good of a person.

CHAPTER TEN

"$\mathcal{I}$t doesn't seem real, does it?" Skyler asked, shaking his head. He sat on a barstool and stared out the French doors at the churning sea. "Gigi's family history would make one hell of a thriller novel."

Iris had to agree. Gigi had explained that her mother had a ring that gave her the gift of life. She could heal terminally ill people. That sounded wonderful, but the power wasn't unlimited. She could only use so much energy and then had to wait while she recovered before she could heal someone else. Gigi's father took care of sending her out on jobs, but eventually she found out he was selling her services to the highest bidder. After that, she'd insisted on helping the less fortunate. When Gigi's dad refused, her mom was so upset by the inequity, she refused to heal anyone else. It was shortly after that when she died trying to destroy the ring.

After explaining her family history, Gigi said the reason she wouldn't allow Iris to pay for Sebastian's services was because her family money had come from exploiting people on their death bed.

"I already have more than I need," Gigi said as she held Iris's hand. "The rest of the money in that trust? I want to do something good with it. Something that will help people who need it. You were fired, leaving you with no income, and now you have these bogus charges to deal with. You shouldn't have to deplete your savings to fight the same type of people who sold life to the highest bidder. Think of it as a grant if that helps. It shouldn't be too hard. I'm in the middle of establishing a legally recognized charitable trust so we can formally help people in the magical community who need it."

"But, Gigi," Iris said. "I think there are other people who probably need the help more than I do."

"Maybe," Gigi replied. "But you're my friend, and I'll be damned if I don't do everything in my power to help you. Got it?"

Iris's heart swelled with gratitude. It was true that she had money in savings to pay Sebastian, but that wasn't going to last long. If she had lawyer bills to pay, then she'd need to start begging someone for a job sooner rather than later. And jobs would be hard to come by while the town was cursed. "Yeah, okay," Iris whispered, overwhelmed by the support of her new friends. "Thank you. I hope Sebastian gives you a good rate."

She chuckled. "As a matter of fact, he does, and I especially like the perk of telling him I've hired him by the hour." Gigi pumped her eyebrows and gave Iris a sly look. "It turns out that stuffing dollar bills in a hot guy's underwear really is a great way to spend an evening."

"Oh gods!" Iris said, playfully stuffing her fingers into her ears. "TMI. TMI!"

"No way," Skyler chimed in. "Tell us more. Like what does he sound like when—"

Gigi slapped her palm over his mouth. "Nope. I'm not

answering that. There is such a thing as privacy. You do realize that, don't you, Skyler?"

After she removed her hand, he made a show of pushing his bottom lip out into a pout. "But it's been so long since I've had a cheap thrill."

They all dissolved into laughter that ended with Skyler making ridiculous faux sex noises that were designed to embarrass both Iris and Gigi. However, that didn't exactly work out for him. When he wouldn't stop, Gigi imitated Meg Ryan in *When Harry Met Sally* as she faked an organism in the middle of a restaurant. And then, right after, Iris offered to stuff money in *his* shorts so he could see for himself just how wonderful it might be. Skyler turned bright red, mumbled something about having promised his mother he'd never become a rent boy, and then took off outside onto the balcony, claiming he desperately needed fresh air.

"Well, that was fun," Gigi said, her eyes sparkling with mischief.

"Who would've thought he'd be so easily embarrassed?" Iris added.

"I think it was the fake orgasm. If a man had done that, he'd have been fine, but for some reason, he gets flustered when I overshare. I don't think he likes the visual that comes with women having sex."

Iris snorted. "So, he's a solid six on the Kinsey scale then?"

"He's a twelve." Gigi winked and jerked her head toward the hallway. "Ready to make some potions?"

"More than ready," Iris said and followed her into what could only be described as an herb sanctuary. The shelves were lined with dozens of jars of herbs while fresh potted plants were lined up near a floor-to-ceiling window, soaking up the afternoon sunlight. She stood at the worktable and basked in the magic tingling over her skin. Instead of being draining, she just felt energized.

Gigi glanced at her and cast her a knowing smile. "It's intoxicating, isn't it?"

Iris nodded. "I don't know why I haven't ever felt this before. It's not like I haven't been around herbs or other witches' workspaces."

"Maybe you're just coming into your powers," Gigi said. "It happens that way for some people. The power lays kind of dormant until suddenly it blossoms into something incredible."

"Is that what happened with you?" Iris asked, wondering what had changed. It seemed strange that she would suddenly be coming into her powers in her late forties.

"Nope. I've always been drawn to earth magic. When I was eighteen, I begged the owner of an apothecary shop in my hometown to let me work there. It's where I learned the basics of everything I do." She pulled a jar of dandelions off the shelf and then reached for her gingerroot. "Ready to make a purifying potion?"

"Purifying? Like purifying one's soul?" she asked with a nervous laugh.

Gigi cackled. "Oh, that would be a fun one. But no, I meant a detox potion. The kind that gives you energy and makes your skin glow."

"Oh, well, that sounds more useful anyway." No wonder Gigi always looked stunning. A purifying potion sounded amazing. Iris definitely could've used that before now.

"You have no idea. Let's get started." Gigi handed her a small knife and a wood cutting board. "I need you to chop up the dandelion stems, and when you have a decent pile, move on to the ginger."

Iris did as she was told and was surprised when a complete calm washed over her. She felt centered and like there was nothing in the world she'd rather be doing than chopping stems. Her muscles relaxed, and her brain stopped racing with all of the events of the past few days. It was glorious.

"You're a natural," Gigi said, watching her.

"At chopping stems?" Iris asked.

"Making potions." She nodded to the pile of already chopped stems. "Look at them. They're glowing with magic already."

Iris's eyes widened. "Did you do that?"

Gigi shook her head. "Nope. I haven't touched them. That's all radiating off you."

"What?" Iris stared at the pile, noting the shimmering magic sparkling over the pieces. She'd really made that happen? After all the years of not being able to tap into her magic, that seemed almost unbelievable. But it was right there before her eyes, making her both elated and filled with emotion. "That's..." she started and then cleared her throat. "Kind of incredible."

"It's brilliant." Gigi grinned at her. "Now do the ginger and then you can put this together."

Iris quickly got to work on the gingerroot. When she was done chopping, Gigi said, "Okay, grab the mini cauldron."

Iris scanned the workstation and let out a small laugh when she spotted the copper cauldron. "Seriously? That's what you use to make your potions?"

"Hey, if you're gonna do something, isn't it best to do it in style?"

"You have a point." Iris grabbed the caldron and placed it in front of her. "Now what?"

"Fill it halfway with distilled water and then add a squeeze of fresh lemon."

When Iris was done, she glanced up at her teacher and waited.

"Now, grab whatever fruit you want from the cooler. Cherries, strawberries, blackberries, whatever flavor you want for this. Crush about a cup full with the mortar and pestle. When you're done, place the caldron on the burner and bring it to a simmer."

Iris got to work, her mind blissfully blank and only focused on the task at hand. It was a little laborious, crushing the fruit by hand, but she didn't mind. She realized it made her feel connected to the concoction.

Once her creation was simmering, Gigi clasped her hands together and said, "Now we're ready for the fun part."

She instructed Iris to add her chopped dandelion stems and ginger. The moment her final ingredients fell into the liquid, the potion turned a gorgeous shade of sunset orange. "Now, repeat after me."

Iris nodded.

"Today I give my thanks to the earth goddess for the gift of magic."

The potion started to bubble as Iris parroted her words.

"Now, use the dropper to extract a small bit of the potion, wait a few seconds for it to cool, and then place a drop on your left palm."

When the liquid landed in Iris's hand, a bolt of magic zapped through her arm. Her hand automatically closed over the drops, and something changed inside of her. She felt strong, completely whole, as if she'd been missing a piece of herself all forty-seven years of her life until that moment.

"Now, ask the earth goddess to bless your potion with the gift to purify," Gigi said.

Iris stared at the potion in the caldron and felt the magic rise up in her chest. And as she asked the earth goddess to do her bidding, magic exploded from her and lit up the room, making everything appear in technicolor. "Whoa."

"I'd say so," Gigi said softly.

Then as the magic faded and the colors returned to normal, Iris focused on her potion and let out a gasp at the forest green-colored tonic. "I used cherries, why did it turn green?"

"It's the dandelions. They always take over and make everything tinged green."

"Tinged? This looks like the emerald forest," Iris said.

Gigi nodded. "It's because of the amount of power you have. You supercharged it."

"Supercharged?" Iris asked, staring down at the potion. "How is that possible? I've never cast a successful spell in my life." Everything about this encounter was surreal, and a crazy thought flashed through her mind. What if she really had been the one to cast the curse over the town and she just didn't know it? Her stomach turned just thinking such a thing. No. Her limbs had been alive with magic while she made the potion. No way would she have failed to notice feeling that kind of power if she'd cursed her entire town. Iris blew out a breath and shook her head, trying to clear the thoughts.

"It must be overwhelming," Gigi said. "If I'd spent my entire life thinking I didn't have magic and then *this* happened, I'd be overwhelmed, too."

"I'm not overwhelmed by *this*." Iris waved a hand at her potion. "At least not that overwhelmed. It's everything else. I feel like I should be investigating everything that is going on instead of basking in the joy of creating potions."

"I'm sure Sebastian is doing everything he can," Gigi said, her brows furrowed together.

"I'm sure he is, too, but there's still that bogus assessment to look into, and I have questions for the Magical Task Force agent I saw in town, not to mention that I really want to know what my ex has to do with all of this. After he showed up trying to get me to confess, I'm sure he's in way over his head. He might be the easiest one to get information from. I know how to push his buttons."

"Sounds like you could use some help," Skyler said from the doorway of the workroom. "Want me to put the gayssips on it?"

"Gayssips? What does that mean?" Iris asked.

"That's what we call the gay network of gossips in this town. I'm telling you, they know everything. And what they don't know, they can usually find out." Skyler gave Iris a conspiratorial look. "Want to know what happened at the Pearsons' get-together last week?"

"Yes!" Gigi said immediately.

"The Pearsons? You mean that older couple who own the gift shop down by the beach?" Iris asked.

"Yes, them. You will die when you hear about Mrs. Pearson's new boytoy."

"Boytoy!" Iris exclaimed. "She's got to be at least seventy. Who's her boytoy?"

"Jeff Ashton. He helps her with her gardening, but it's not the flower beds he's plowing," Skyler said with a snicker.

Jeff Ashton was a retired landscaper who was probably still in his fifties. "Well, as long as Mr. Pearson doesn't have a problem with it, then I say more power to her. Imagine the stamina he must have compared to her husband," Iris said, knowing Mr. Pearson just turned seventy-seven.

"Oh, you don't know the half of it," Skyler said, laughing. "He's plowing his best friend's widow and her brother too."

"At the same time?" Gigi exclaimed.

"No, no. Apparently he has some limits." Chuckling, Skyler scratched his chin. "While I'm not into sharing in any way—gods, if Pete stepped out on me, I'd strangle him. Anyway, as I was saying, sharing isn't for me, but I guess the variety is working for the Pearsons. I've never seen a couple appear to be so happy and content when they're out and about together."

Iris couldn't disagree. "They always do seem really cute together. But what does this have to do with getting information about the curse and who's really behind it?"

"Oh, just you wait, Iris. You'd be surprised at how loose some lips are after orgasms. Just leave it to me. I'll get the network on it and let you know what they find." He waved his fingers at them and called a goodbye as he disappeared down the hall.

"I really like him," Iris told Gigi.

Gigi snorted. "Yeah, me too. Now drink your potion so we can see just how effective it really is."

Iris poured some of the thick green potion into a small glass, raised it, and said, "Cheers."

CHAPTER ELEVEN

*I*ris was still on a magical high when she walked through the front door of her little cottage. An unfamiliar beep sounded as she shut the door, and she startled for a moment before she remembered the alarm that had been put in earlier that day. She pulled out her phone and looked for the code she'd saved and typed it in. The flashing light went out, and the monitor went silent.

"You're going to reset that, aren't you?" her mother asked from the kitchen doorway. Her hair was pulled up into a haphazard bun, and she was wearing gray sweatpants with a matching gray sweatshirt. It was the most dressed down Iris had seen her in over twenty years.

"Why?" Iris glanced at the closed door and then made a show of turning the dead bolt.

"It doesn't take that much for witches to break through door locks."

Iris hated to admit it, but her mother was right. Score one for Katheryn. She shrugged and turned back to the alarm, scrolling through the settings until she had the perimeter set. "There. Better?"

"Yes. As a matter of fact, it is better." She waved at her daughter. "Come into the kitchen. I want to talk to you for a bit."

When Iris didn't respond, Katheryn blew out a breath. "Come on, Iris. I made sugar cookies."

"You made cookies?" Iris asked, shocked. "Since when do you bake?"

Katheryn let out an irritated huff. "You make it sound like I've never lifted a finger in the kitchen. I've always baked. But when you were young, I just didn't have time."

That's because her mother was too busy going from relationship to relationship while working twelve to fourteen-hour days. Iris was lucky if she saw her mom for a half hour before the nanny of the week demanded lights out. "What else do you bake?" Iris asked, intensely curious if she actually did spend time in the kitchen lately.

"Look for yourself." She nodded at the glass baking dish on the counter.

Iris peered at it and let out a gasp. "Did you make lasagna?"

Katheryn nodded.

Drool immediately pooled on Iris's tongue. The one thing that her mother had always done well was lasagna. Iris immediately reached for a spatula, but just before she cut into it, she asked, "This is for dinner tonight, right? You didn't make this for some potluck somewhere that I don't know about?"

"A potluck? Here in Premonition Pointe? Where would I be going for something like that? Especially considering the streets are practically empty."

"I don't know. I just didn't want to get ahead of myself."

Katheryn grabbed a couple of plates from the cabinets and

said, "Load them up. I'm starving after all the work I did today."

Iris glanced around her spotless kitchen and was impressed. Not only had her mother cooked, but she'd cleaned, too. That was a first. Growing up, it was always Iris's job to clean the kitchen, no matter who created the mess.

They took their plates to the small table in the breakfast nook, but before Katheryn sat down, she grabbed a bottle of red wine and filled two glasses.

Iris had to admit that coming home to a freshly baked lasagna and a nice red wine didn't suck. Not in the least. "Thank you, Mom. This was really thoughtful."

"You're welcome, sweetie. After the past few days you've had, I just wanted to do something nice for you." Her mother took a nice long sip of her wine and then forked a piece of her lasagna. "I also made chicken taco soup. I figured it would help if you had leftovers to heat up."

"Wow. That was above and beyond." Iris reached out and squeezed her mother's hand. "You even did the dishes. If I had any money, I'd hire you."

"Speaking of money, how are you paying that lawyer of yours? If you'd just let me—"

Iris held her hand up and did her best to not snap at her mother. "I've got it, Mom. Sebastian is doing a fine job, and the bills are handled. You don't have to worry about it."

"I'm going to worry regardless. I'm your mother, after all," Katheryn said, staring Iris in the eye.

"Really? Where was all that worry when you were working sixteen hours a day when I was in junior high and stranded at school for hours every day before someone finally came to pick me up?" She hadn't meant to lash out at her mother. The words just flew out of her mouth without her permission.

Katheryn sighed. "Do we have to do this now?"

"Nope." Iris stood up, taking her plate with her. "We never have to do it. I guess that's why we never talk about what's really wrong with this relationship. But don't worry. We don't have to do it tonight either." Iris grabbed her wine glass and started to make her way out of the kitchen with her dinner in hand.

"Wait!" Katheryn jumped up, took the plate and the glass, and put them both back on the table. "Don't go. I really would like to talk to you."

Iris raised a skeptical eyebrow. There was a bite in her tone when she asked, "Is this one of those conversations where you talk and I get to listen?"

Her mother sighed heavily. "No. I want to really talk."

There was a sincerity in her mother's tone that Iris hadn't heard before, and that realization helped her drop her defensiveness as she took a seat at the table. "Okay. Let's talk."

Katheryn stared at her plate of food for a long moment before pushing it away and giving Iris her full attention. "I know I made mistakes when you were younger. A lot of them."

Iris blinked. That wasn't a statement she'd heard from her before. "Okay."

"I know I owe you an apology. Hell, probably dozens of apologies. But you have to know that the reason I worked so hard was because I was trying to provide for us. All of those men in my life… They weren't reliable. I wanted to make sure you had a stable life, and the only way I could do that was to work crazy hours."

It wasn't the only way, but Iris kept her mouth shut. Now wasn't the time to remind her mother that she could've worked a regular nine-to-five job. That she didn't have to be the start-up entrepreneur not once, but twice. Sure, she'd manage to make a good living both times, but it meant being an absentee mother to a daughter who'd lost her father early in life.

"I know what you're thinking," Katheryn said with a wry smile.

"You do not."

She barked out a laugh. "Yes, I do. You're wishing I would've gone to work for someone else. That I hadn't been tied to my companies and that I'd made it a priority to take time off so we could spend more time together."

Busted. Iris was thinking all of those things. She'd never understood people who wanted kids but then didn't make it a priority to be there for them while they were growing up. "Maybe some of it," she conceded.

"All of it," Katheryn insisted with a small, weak smile. "It's okay. I know I was MIA, and I want to apologize for that. Only please understand it wasn't because I didn't want to spend time with my daughter. I was trying to build something for us that would last."

At least she'd done that. Built something that would last. While both of the companies she'd started had failed, the one she'd gotten in the divorce from her fifth and final husband had been another story altogether. She'd taken possession of a failing spa that specialized in various water treatments, such as underwater massage, mineral spas, and sauna detoxes. Because she was a talented water witch, Katheryn had managed to turn it into a sort of holistic haven for those with chronic pain. As soon as word got out, her spa took off and she'd never looked back. Now there were franchises owned by other water witches in most major cities across the US and in Europe. These days Katheryn didn't run her own store the way she had when Iris was in high school. Now she was a corporate executive who owned a handful of her own stores that were managed by her original assistant manager while Katheryn spent her time overseeing the franchises.

The venture was a complete success, and Katheryn wasn't lacking for much.

Except maybe a meaningful relationship with her daughter.

"Okay," Iris said. "You have a successful company now. You did what you set out to do. That must make you happy."

"No, dammit!" Katheryn brought her fist down on the table hard enough to make their dishes rattle. "I'm not happy. My daughter hates me, doesn't respect me, and never answers my calls. Why did I spend all those years building something for us when you don't want any part of it?"

All of the air left Iris's lungs. She sucked in a fortifying breath and stared her mother in the eye. "I don't hate you."

Her mother's eyebrows rose in surprise. "You could've fooled me."

Iris sighed. "Like I said, I don't hate you. But I do resent it when you—"

"You resent me?" she cried, standing up and leaning over the table in a domineering manor.

"Mother! If you want to have this conversation, then you have to let me talk. This, right here, is why I get resentful." Iris placed both hands on the table, consciously trying to keep from curling them into fists. "You don't listen to me."

"I listen," she said quietly as she sat back in her chair, her shoulders slumped in acquiescence.

"Sure you do," Iris said dryly. "I suppose that's why you kept trying to fire Sebastian, even though I'd already told you he was my lawyer and I wasn't going to use yours."

"I was just trying to help. Just like I tried to help when I went grocery shopping for you today, cleaned your house, which you didn't even notice, and cooked a couple of dinners. Not to mention the fact that I filled your cookie jar."

"You... shopped and cleaned?" Iris glanced around, really taking things in. She'd noticed the clean kitchen, but everything else? Iris got up and inspected the living room and then the bathrooms. Her mother was right. Everything was sparkling clean, and the place smelled faintly of lemon. When she returned to the kitchen, she opened the cabinets and right away spotted a bag of fancy coffee. Tears stung her eyes, and she turned back to her mother. "You really did go all out today, didn't you?"

She shrugged one shoulder. "Like I said, I just wanted to make things easier for you."

Iris took her seat and scooted closer to her mother. After wrapping her hands around both of her mother's, she said, "Thank you, Mom. All of this..." she nodded toward the kitchen and then toward the living room, "was really thoughtful. Those are the kinds of things that really do help me. And I really appreciate it. More than you know, actually. But the other stuff... Barging in and trying to take over? Trying to fire my lawyer or order people around who are doing work for me, that's not okay. It's overbearing and makes me feel as if you think I can't handle my own life."

"I don't think that!" She extracted one of her hands and wiped at her eyes. "You're... amazing. You were elected mayor and kicked that bastard Tom to the curb the moment you realized he was no good. I wish I'd have had that kind of courage a couple of times in my life."

"Mom, you dumped not one, but two abusive assholes," Iris said, referring to her first and third husbands. Iris had laid into her earlier about all of her relationships, but the truth was that while Katheryn certainly wasn't blameless in her failed marriages, those two had fooled both Iris and her mother. It wasn't until after they'd married her that they showed their true colors with their fists. One was a mean drunk, and the other had anger management issues he'd managed to hide long enough to put a ring on her finger. Katheryn hadn't wasted a moment throwing them out and filing restraining orders.

As for her other three marriages, one left her for his first wife. One didn't like all the time she spent at work and tried to get her to be a housewife. And the final one... Well, that was the one everyone thought might last. Iris still didn't know why they broke up. He was there one day, and the next day he wasn't. But her mom got the spa business in the deal, so not everything was lost.

"I made a lot of mistakes with men in my life, sweetheart," Katheryn said. "I just want you to learn from my mistakes."

As if Iris hadn't already. She'd spent years afraid of commitment. Then she'd met Tom. It was really too bad that he'd betrayed her in more ways than one. It was unlikely that Iris would trust easily again. Kade's image flashed in her mind. Her heart skipped a beat, and she wanted to punch herself for letting her feelings run away from her. Trying to date someone while she had criminal charges hanging over her head was a terrible idea.

She shook her head slightly, trying to dislodge his image, and gave her mom a reassuring smile. "Don't worry. I've seen enough to know how to protect my heart."

"That's not really what I meant," Katheryn said with a frown.

"I know, Mom." She squeezed her hand again. "Don't worry about me. After Tom's BS, I'm not looking to get serious with anyone, so there's not much to worry about."

Katheryn turned to look out the window toward Kade's house and then back at Iris. "Are you sure about that?"

Was she? No. Not at all. But she wasn't going to tell her mom that. The confession would come with hours of advice, and right then she really just wanted to crawl into bed. "Listen, Mom. It's late. I'm going to hit the sack. Thanks again for everything. Your help today, it was perfect."

Iris stood and was picking up her plate to take it to the sink when Katheryn stopped her.

"I've got this. Go on. You look really tired. You need your rest if you're going to get rid of those bags under your eyes before your date on Saturday morning."

The comment was so flip, Iris was certain her mother hadn't even realized just how rude it sounded. Instead of telling her mother off, she just nodded and said, "Good night, Mom. See you in the morning."

"Night, sweetie. Be sure to use that aging cream I left on the counter for you."

Gritting her teeth, Iris said nothing as she disappeared into her bedroom and did her best to not imagine her mother being eaten by crows.

CHAPTER TWELVE

*I*ris woke with an odd sense of unease. She sat up in her bed and glanced around, trying to understand the source of her discomfort. The overly bright morning sun blazed through her window, illuminating her room. She groaned. The position of the sun indicated she'd slept late. Maybe that was the reason she felt so off. Normally she was an early riser. But after her talk with her mother the night before, she'd had trouble falling asleep. She hadn't been able to stop thinking about her mother's apology.

Honestly, Iris never thought she'd see the day when her mother would even talk about the past much less take some responsibility for their strained relationship. And as much as she wanted to believe that it was the catalyst for a better relationship between the two of them, she was worried that it would backfire and, in a week or so, Iris's honesty would come back to bite her in the ass.

It wouldn't be the first time that Iris had been honest with her mother about her feelings only to have her mother use her words against her a few weeks later for reasons Iris would never understand.

Maybe this time would be different. All she could do was wait and see and hope for the best.

After a shower, Iris pulled on a pair of jeans and a T-shirt and stuffed her feet into a pair of athletic shoes. Her only goals for the rest of the morning were to down some coffee and then take a walk on the beach to clear her head.

When Iris made it into her kitchen, her mother was nowhere to be found. She hadn't left a note either, but that wasn't unusual for Katheryn. She'd never been the forthcoming type. The idea that Iris might wonder where she was probably hadn't even occurred to her. Iris was used to it though, and just went about her business.

Once she had her coffee in a travel mug, Iris grabbed a sweatshirt and headed for the door. Just before she opened it, there was a knock, startling her. She jerked back and almost dropped her mug. A bit sloshed out of the opening and landed on the tile floor. Iris scowled and stepped over the mess to open the door.

A petite woman in a crisp uniform stood on the porch with a clipboard in her hand. "Iris Martin?"

Iris's stomach churned on the small amount of acidic coffee in her belly. The plain black uniform with one silver star on the collar was the distinct uniform of a Magical Task Force agent. Dammit. There went her walk. "Yes, I'm Iris Martin. And you are?"

"Ginny Stevens." The agent held her hand out to Iris. "I've heard a lot about you over the years. I wish we were meeting under better circumstances."

Iris shook her hand, wishing the same thing. "I suppose

you're here to follow up on the charges the city has filed against me."

She nodded. "That and I'd like to take a look at the area where the spell was cast."

"Good," Iris said, happy that someone from the MTF was going to look at the evidence left behind from the spell that was cast on her property. That would be one step closer to clearing her name. Since Iris had nothing to do with that spell, her magical signature wouldn't be linked to it, and to have a report like that in her case file would make the case against her fall apart. Iris opened the door and waved her in. "Do you want some coffee? I'm happy to make a fresh pot."

"No, I'm good," Ginny said with a short nod. She was glancing around with a keen eye, and Iris was pleased to see that she was all business. It wasn't long before Iris knew without a doubt that Ginny was one hundred percent a professional. She wasted no time getting down to business.

"Can we sit and talk for a few minutes?" Ginny asked Iris. "I'd like to ask you a few questions."

"Sure." Iris led her to the kitchen table and again offered her something to drink.

"No thanks. I bring my own. It's safer that way." She gave Iris a faint smile and reached into her bag, pulling out a water bottle.

Iris grimaced, realizing she did that just in case she was dealing with someone who might be trying to actively curse her. She took a seat across from the woman and said, "Well, if you change your mind, just let me know."

"Thank you for the offer. That's kind." She rummaged around in her satchel and produced a legal pad. Then she set her phone on the table, her finger hovering over the screen.

"This is going to be recorded. I'm required to inform you, though your consent is not required."

"Got it." Iris was familiar with the procedure. This wasn't her first rodeo with the Magical Task Force, though it was the first time that she was a suspect. Just the reminder that someone had tried to pin this crime on her made her angry all over again.

Ginny asked for her name, address, and a bunch of other identifying information before inquiring about Tom. "You're divorced?"

Iris nodded. "He was involved in some drug activity that I was not aware of. When everything came to light, I told him it was over and he moved out. I wouldn't say it was an amicable divorce, but we managed to keep it civil. Or at least I thought so until he showed up at the jail and tried to get me to confess to something I didn't do."

The agent raised a curious eyebrow. "He wanted you to confess to... what exactly?"

"Cursing the town," Iris said, waving a hand. Wasn't that obvious? She was sure it was, but the agent would want to get that on record. "He said the DA was willing to cut me a sweet deal if I just confessed to the crime. And then he insinuated that life would get worse for me if I didn't."

"I take it that means you're not going to confess?" she asked.

"Of course not," Iris said hotly, leaning in closer to stare the agent in the eyes. "I don't have the talent to cast a curse like that. And even if I did, I'm the last person who'd curse Premonition Pointe. I've done nothing but try to help the town grow during my tenure as mayor. Why in the world would I want to destroy that?"

"Because they fired you?" Ginny prompted.

Iris knew the woman was only doing her job, but it still

pissed her off. She sat back in her chair and crossed her arms over her chest defiantly. "Let me be super clear here. I did not, nor would I ever, cast any curse to hurt Premonition Pointe or any of its residents. Besides, I've never been good at magic. There's no way I could've pulled that off. And I wasn't even here when it happened. Just ask Kade from next door. We were at the corner café when the shit hit the fan."

"I'll do that," Ginny said with a nod as she made more notes. When she looked up, she continued her questioning. "I have it in my notes that your mother is a powerful water witch."

"That's true. She seems to thrive off the sea. That's not unusual though. Isn't that why the coast is a magnet for so many witches?"

"I didn't say it was unusual," Ginny said evenly. "I was just clarifying for my notes. Does she use her power frequently?"

"Yes. She owns a therapeutic spa business. The treatments wouldn't be nearly as effective if she didn't use her magic." Iris lowered her arms and rolled her shoulders, trying to relax. It really was a shame she hadn't gotten to take that walk she'd wanted. It was likely she'd be less jittery if she'd gotten some steps in. She shifted in her chair, trying to keep her butt from going numb.

Ginny put her pen down for a moment and took a long swig of water. When she was done, her skin started to glow a bit, making Iris eye her water bottle. She was certain Ginny had just swallowed some sort of potion instead of pure water. She was about to ask her about it when Ginny filled the silence. "Does your mom use magic regularly outside of work?"

It shouldn't have, but the question took Iris off guard a bit. She blinked, thought back to her childhood, and grimaced. "Yes, she does. Or at least she used to. She had a habit of slipping people memory potions when she wasn't getting her way. Nothing that wiped memories or anything, more like potions that had the power of suggestion. She might also have dabbled in love potions for a while, even though they weren't very effective." Iris hated that she was spilling her mother's secrets, but if the MTF agent detected that she was lying, that would only hurt her case.

"Water witches have never been very good at making love potions," she remarked as she continued to make notes. "Herbs are better for that."

Iris nodded.

"Anything else?" Ginny asked.

"Not that I can recall." Iris knew her mother was always trying other things, but she couldn't remember the specifics. None of it was terribly harmful anyway.

"Okay. I just need a list of names of everyone you've interacted with over the past week."

"Why?" Iris frowned. "Are you going to interrogate them, too?" Her heart sank at the idea that they were likely going to interview Kade. They hadn't even had their first date yet, and he was going to be interrogated just for being a friendly neighbor. The hope she'd been harboring for a possible relationship with him vanished. Why would anyone want to date her? She was a hot mess at the moment. Not a good way to start out.

"I just need to corroborate what you've told me. That's all." She waited patiently until Iris sighed and started listing off all of her friends as well as all the city officials she'd come in contact with since they'd arrested her. When she mentioned speaking with Julie a few times, Ginny paused her notetaking and stared at Iris.

"Julie Lairds? The mayor's assistant?" she asked, sounding surprised.

"Yes. Julie was my assistant before they fired me. We're friendly," Iris said casually as if she and Julie were the type of friends to do lunch occasionally. They weren't, but Iris wouldn't rule it out. She liked Julie.

"Did you know Mayor Howell fired her yesterday?"

Iris let out a small gasp. "He did? Why?"

"He's worried about internal leaks." The agent stared pointedly at Iris. "You wouldn't know anything about that, would you?"

Swallowing hard, Iris shook her head. Had her phone call about the assessment notices been the reason Julie was without a job?

"What aren't you telling me?" Ginny asked.

Should she tell her about the bill that Skyler had gotten? She could, but she didn't want Tad to hear that she was poking around about it until she had some sort of proof that it was fraudulent. It was her one chance to show the town that Tad was a terrible choice. Even if Iris never held the position again, she wanted someone in the role of mayor who cared about the residents of Premonition Pointe. "Nothing, I'm just surprised," Iris said. "Julie is a great assistant. I feel bad for her."

"Sometimes leaders have to make choices that aren't easy," Ginny said, capping her pen and stuffing it back into her bag. "I'm sure you made many while you were mayor."

"Of course." Iris stood, ready for the agent to leave. She was all for being cooperative, but she didn't handle condescension well. "Do you have what you need?"

Ginny studied Iris for a long moment until her lips curved into a tiny self-satisfied smile.

What the hell was that about?

The smile vanished, and Ginny was all business again when she announced she'd be checking the house both inside and out for magical remnants and then would be on her way.

"Fine." Iris sat at her table, watching as the agent made her way outside and started scanning her backyard with a magical detector. She was dying to call Julie to find out what happened, but refrained. Iris didn't want to give the agent any ammunition to use against her, even if it shouldn't be a problem or a surprise that she'd be friends with someone she'd worked with for years. The truth was, she *was* pumping Julie for information, but that information didn't have to do with the curse. She was certain that if Julie knew anything about who'd cast it, she'd have already told someone. The woman had too much integrity for that. It was that bill that Iris suspected was pure extortion that she needed Julie's help with.

Iris's phone buzzed, distracting her from the agent who was pacing her yard. She glanced down and saw it was a message from Sebastian.

I have good news. I'm on my way over.

Iris immediately typed back. *Have they found who did this to Premonition Pointe?*

No. I'll be there in five. Will explain then.

Iris got up and moved to a chair on her front porch where her knee bounced with anticipation. The door of Kade's house burst open, startling her, followed by a small fluffy dog bolting out of the house and straight over to Iris. BeeBee barked once and then sailed onto Iris's lap, her tongue going a mile a minute as she slathered Iris's face with kisses.

CHAPTER THIRTEEN

"Hey there, Houdini," Iris said with a laugh when she realized that Kade hadn't followed BeeBee out the door. "How did you manage to get that door open all by yourself?"

The dog's body wiggled uncontrollably as she put her front two paws on Iris's shoulders and the kisses intensified.

Iris threw her head back and laughed, relieved to have something else to focus on other than the MTF agent still gathering evidence on her property. "Were you just waiting for your opportunity to bust out?" Iris glanced over at Kade's empty driveway. It appeared her neighbor wasn't even home. She reached into her pocket and grabbed her phone. After awkwardly typing out a text to Kade to let him know his dog escaped and that she was taking care of her, she hit Send.

His return text was almost immediate. *BeeBee got out of the house? How?*

She busted the door open. Not sure. Don't worry. I'll close it and keep her here with me until you get home.

Thank you. I should be home in a few hours. Just finishing a piece for Lucas. I could grab dinner as a thank you for dog sitting.

Iris smiled, already looking forward to spending time with him. *You know that's not necessary, right?*

Maybe not, but I'm going to do it anyway. Any special requests?

Nope. Surprise me. I don't have any allergies, so make it interesting. She added a winkie-face emoji and smirked at her phone as she sent it.

Oh, a challenge. You're on. And again, thanks for watching BeeBee.

Don't mention it. She stuffed her phone back into her pocket and stood. "Come on, BeeBee. Let's go put your house back in order."

Iris walked down the steps of her porch and glanced back when BeeBee didn't follow her. "What's up, baby girl? Too lazy to make the journey with me?"

The fluffy dog went from sitting to lying flat on her stomach, her paws wide and her head flattened on the porch.

"I guess that answers my question," she said with a laugh. "Fine. You stay right here. I'll take care of your dad's house."

When BeeBee didn't move a muscle, Iris walked next door, peeked in at the immaculate house, and wondered how exactly the man kept his place so pristine with a dog living there. She was about to close the door when she spotted a couple of dog bowls in the entry way. One was filled with water and the other had a bit of food in it. Right. BeeBee might actually need those. She grabbed the dishes and the leash hanging on a hook by the door, closed up the house, and returned to the dog still lying patiently on her porch.

"Well, I guess you were serious about hanging out on my porch," Iris said, placing the dishes nearby.

BeeBee raised her head long enough to glance at the bowls

and then lowered it again and rolled onto her back, exposing her belly.

Iris laughed and squatted down to pet her.

The sound of a car approaching made her glance up to find Sebastian parking his SUV behind a plain black sedan. He smiled widely and waved as he darted up to the porch. He glanced at BeeBee. "Hey, sweetheart. What are you doing here?"

"She decided she was done sitting at home for a while and busted out. She's visiting for a few hours." She waved at the chairs behind her. "Want to have a seat?"

"Sure. Are you joining me?" he asked, a trace of amusement in his tone.

"In a minute." She continued to pet BeeBee's tummy until the dog turned her head and gave her arm a lick. "Ahh, thanks, sweetie. I appreciate you, too." After patting the pup on the head, she retreated to the chairs and turned her attention to her lawyer. "Okay, spill. What is it you have to tell me?"

He grinned. "After laying out the known facts in your case to the DA and suggesting there were mitigating circumstances that made this case ripe for an Internal Affairs investigation, he agreed to drop the charges."

"What? Seriously?" she cried.

"Seriously. You're in the clear."

"Not so fast," Ginny said, walking around from the side of the house and up the steps to the porch. Her lips thinned into a straight line as she stared at Iris. "I've uncovered some troubling issues that could put you back in legal trouble."

Sebastian stood abruptly, stepping in front of Iris as if to shield her as he addressed Ginny. "I'm sorry. We haven't met. Care to introduce yourself?"

"Ginny Stevens. I'm an agent from the Magical Task Force. And you are?"

He crossed his arms over his chest and stiffened. "Sebastian Knight, Iris's lawyer."

She nodded. "Good. Care to go inside so we can talk?"

Iris gritted her teeth. She just wanted the agent to spit out whatever it was that she'd found.

Sebastian glanced at Iris. "Is that okay with you?"

"I guess so," she said with a sigh. "It's better to know than to be blindsided, right?" Without waiting for a reply, she got up, grabbed BeeBee's dishes, and whistled for the dog to follow her. BeeBee stayed on her heels, and when Iris took a seat at her table, BeeBee curled up at her feet. She reached down and patted the dog's head. "Good girl, BeeBee baby."

Sebastian followed Ginny in, but opted to keep standing even as the agent took a seat across from Iris.

Ginny glanced at him. "You're not going to sit?"

He grabbed the back of one of the chairs and shook his head. "I'd rather stand."

She let out a small sigh, a rare display of something other than cool professionalism. "I'm not the enemy."

"Maybe not, but it sounds like you're the person standing in the way of this case against my client being completely dropped," Sebastian said, narrowing his eyes at her. "That means you're not exactly a friend either."

"Sebastian," Iris said, suddenly tired. "She's just doing her job." Iris gave him a weak smile. "I appreciate your support, but why don't we listen to what she has to say before we get hostile."

"Hostile?" Ginny asked, her eyebrows disappearing under her bangs.

"It's a figure of speech," Iris said, wishing she had another cup of coffee just to have something to do with her hands.

"Alright," Ginny said, getting down to business. "There are a couple of things that I have to put into my report that are concerning. First, your backyard has been cleansed of magic."

Iris sat up straight and then leaned forward with her elbows on the table. "What do you mean my backyard has been cleansed of magic?" She turned to Sebastian. "Was that part of the sweep you guys did?"

"Sweep?" Ginny asked.

Sebastian gave Iris a pointed look, indicating that she should stop talking.

A sinking feeling landed in Iris's gut. Oops. Had she just messed up? Surely sweeping her house for bugs wasn't against any rule, was it? She had a right to her privacy and to remove any cameras that had been installed without her permission. Though she suspected this was more about making sure that there were no questions about unsavory activity at her house. She clamped her mouth shut and decided to let Sebastian handle the rest of the meeting.

"I had a security team check the house for bugs and hidden cameras. After the curse was cast in her backyard, I wanted to make sure nothing else nefarious was going on," he said. "But we did not do any sort of cleansing of magic in the backyard. That's not even in our wheelhouse."

"But it's in hers," Ginny said, nodding to Iris.

"No, it isn't," Iris said automatically.

"Iris, please let me handle this," Sebastian said, giving her another pained look.

"Sorry." She reached down and picked up BeeBee, needing something to focus on before she lost her mind. The dog settled in her lap and instantly relaxed as Iris stroked her ears.

"As Iris indicated, her magic isn't nearly strong enough to cleanse a site that had been the source of a curse," Sebastian insisted. "In fact, it wasn't until after the curse happened and she enlisted help from the town coven that she even realized she had usable magic at all. Does a couple of days of dabbling in magic seem like enough time to develop such a complex skill?"

"That brings me to the second thing I have to put in the report. When she was questioned by the detective on this case, Iris indicated that she didn't have the power or ability to cast such a curse. But it's obvious Iris has more than minimal magic," Ginny insisted. "It's radiating off her like a freaking magic fountain."

Iris glanced down at her bare arms as if she were going to see something. All she saw was her hair standing up as if there was an electrical charge in the air. Being that they lived on the coast, that wasn't exactly unusual.

"I don't see anything," Sebastian said.

Ginny pulled out a small scanner gun, pointed it at Iris, and pressed a button. A light flashed red, and the scanner started making an obnoxiously loud beeping noise. She made a note of whatever the reading was and then started to turn back to Sebastian. But before she met his gaze, she stared at Iris with her mouth hanging open. "Holy shit. I've never seen that happen before."

Iris looked down at herself and let out a gasp when she spotted a golden light outlining her body. She sat completely still, watching as the magic rippled just above her skin. "What is that?"

"It's a revealing spell, designed to bring your magic to the surface. It shows how powerful you are," Ginny said. "You, Iris

Hartsen, are a very powerful witch. I'm not sure why you and your lawyer are claiming otherwise."

Iris opened her mouth to defend herself, but Sebastian cut her off. "No matter how powerful she is, the fact remains that up until a few days ago, Iris didn't even know she had power lurking beneath the surface. You can check her employee records with the city and see that she never used magic for her job. A background report will reveal she's never been cited for using magic unlawfully. And if you want to look even harder, perhaps check her school records. You'll find that she was a bright student who didn't engage in any of the extracurriculars that involved magic. That's common for those from magical families that for some reason weren't blessed with the same amount of power as their parents or siblings."

"So, you're saying that Iris just came into her power," Ginny said with a nod. "That happens sometimes. Especially to women who are starting menopause. Hormones change, and magic is unlocked."

"Really?" Iris's hands were shaking. She knew she wasn't responsible for the curse or anything else that had gone on in her backyard. But if the agent put it in her report, there was no telling what the DA and Tad would try to do with that.

"Oh, yeah. We see it all the time. Once the facial hair starts growing, look out. The magic is just as strong as the hot flashes." Ginny fanned her face as if she were having a hot flash right then and there. Though Iris was certain the woman wouldn't know her way around a hot flash even if it slapped her across the face.

"Hand fans don't do shit for hot flashes," Iris muttered. "They're more like having literal fireballs trying to burn your skin off. It's gonna take a full-on HVAC system to touch one of those."

The agent chuckled to herself. "That's consistent with what I've heard. But since it sounds like you know what you're talking about when it comes to hot flashes, I'd say you're one of the lucky witches who likely came into your magic because of the hormone changes. If I were you, I'd get my levels checked just to make sure nothing goes haywire."

"Sure," Iris said, not wanting to be rude, but also trying to let Sebastian handle the rest of the visit.

Sebastian finally sat and rested his elbows on the table. He leaned closer to the agent and said, "Look, just because someone swept Iris's backyard of remnant magic and she may be coming into her own, that doesn't change the fact that there is no evidence that she did this. It's likely that whoever cast the spell learned that there'd be a paranormal investigation and did what they could to cover their tracks. Meanwhile, Iris has a solid alibi for the time period when the curse was cast, and if you talk to the coven, I'm sure they will confirm that she is just starting to learn about her abilities."

"That may all be true, Mr. Knight, but I'm still obligated to put what I found here in a report," she said.

"It doesn't make you obligated to draw conclusions though." Sebastian turned his attention toward the back door. "Did it ever occur to you that it's likely the Premonition Pointe police cleansed the magic out there?"

"Why would they do that?" Ginny asked, sounding genuinely curious.

Sebastian shook his head. "I don't know, Agent Stevens. Tell me why the city council ousted her when she'd done nothing but improve almost every aspect of this town during her tenure. Why did they coerce her ex-husband into trying to scare her into taking a deal? But most importantly, if they had any concrete evidence on her, why would they drop the charges today when I threatened to get Internal Affairs involved?"

A tiny smile curved the agent's lips, and then just as suddenly the smile was gone. She cleared her throat. "Obviously I don't have the answer to that. Thank you for your candor. I'm not here to make judgments. But I did want to warn you that I have to put everything I've found in my report." She glanced at Iris. "Can you think of anyone who might've cleansed the magic from your backyard?"

Iris automatically shook her head, but as soon as she did, a sharp pain stabbed her in the stomach as realization washed over her.

There was only one person who would take matters like that into her own hands.

Iris's mother, Katheryn West.

CHAPTER FOURTEEN

"None of that evidence is conclusive," Sebastian said as soon as the MTF agent left.

"I know," Iris said, picking BeeBee up off her lap and carrying her into the living room. She curled up at the end of her couch and closed her eyes with BeeBee beside her. "It sure does make me look guilty though."

Sebastian had followed her into the living room and was pacing now. "I think someone from the department did it."

"Why?" Iris rubbed her temple, trying to ease the ache that had formed in the last half hour. She'd gone from the charges being dropped to some sort of weird limbo through no fault of her own.

"Think about it. If someone from the new administration cast the curse, they'd certainly want to cover that up. And by doing it this way, it makes you look like you were covering your own tracks."

Iris snorted out a laugh. "That would make me the dumbest criminal in the history of the world. Why would I cast the curse from my backyard and risk being a suspect in the first place?"

"Newbie mistake?" he suggested.

"Dammit. Yeah, that would work as an argument."

Sebastian took a seat in the chair across from her. "It's an argument they can use, but it doesn't hold up without actual evidence. I'd feel better if we could prove who wiped the magic from your yard."

Iris swallowed.

Sebastian's eyes widened. "Do you know who did it?"

She shook her head slowly then said, "I don't *know*, but I have an idea of who it could have been."

"Tell me and I'll check it out."

He already had his phone out, ready to type in a name, when she said, "My mother spent the day baking and cleaning yesterday. She kept saying she wanted to help me. And I'm not totally sure she believes that I didn't cast the curse. I wouldn't be surprised if this was her."

"Dammit!" Sebastian got to his feet and started to pace. "If that's proven, it will be bad for our case."

"I doubt she'll admit it, if that helps at all." Iris desperately wanted to lie down on the couch and just sleep the afternoon away. How had her life fallen apart so quickly? It was more than overwhelming.

"I'll interview her myself," Sebastian said. "When will she be back?"

"I have no idea. Katheryn comes and goes as she pleases."

Sebastian nodded, typed something on his phone, and then turned back to her. "You look beat. I'm going to get out of here and let you rest. In the meantime, I'll do everything in my power to try and keep them from charging you again."

Iris let her gaze drift to his. "Do you think they will?"

"They'll likely try. The lead officer was pissed when he learned that the DA was dropping the charges, so it's best we be prepared for anything."

She let out a groan. "All right. We'll just have to figure out who did this before they can build a bogus case against me."

"Iris," Sebastian said, a gentle warning in his tone. "Please be careful. You don't want to give them any more ammunition to use against you."

"I know." She let out a sigh. "It's just that I have to do *something*."

"No, you don't. I'll hire an investigator to get to the bottom of this." He started to move toward the door.

Iris processed what he'd said. "That's not a normal thing when paying a lawyer, is it?"

"No, not usually. But this case calls for an exception."

"All right," Iris said with a nod. "But I'm paying for that. Not Gigi or her foundation, understand? I can't just be using all of those resources when I know other people need them more than I do."

He opened his mouth and started to say something as he shook his head.

Iris raised her hand to stop him and said, "Forget it. Those are my terms."

Sebastian paused for a moment then nodded. "All right. It's a deal."

* * *

IRIS WOKE to someone caressing her cheek. The soft touch was so nice, she leaned in, greedy for more before her eyes flew open and she jerked back, startled at having someone invading her space. "Holy crap! How did you get in here? The door was locked and the alarm was set."

"Sorry!" Kade said, holding both hands up. "Your mom was here. She let me in just as she was leaving. I didn't mean to startle you. You just looked so peaceful, I wanted to give you a moment to ease into consciousness."

Wow. She'd been so out of it she hadn't even heard her mom come in or leave apparently. "Did she say where she was going?"

"She said she had dinner plans."

Iris frowned. She really wished her mother had woken her or stayed in for once. They had things to talk about. Specifically, she needed to find out if Katheryn had tried to *help* her by cleansing the magic from her yard. Suddenly a new worry settled in her gut. Who exactly was her mother having dinner with? Was she out there causing more trouble for Iris or just herself? She squeezed her eyes shut and tried to push the thoughts from her mind. Worrying about it wasn't going to help. She just needed to make sure she had a talk with her mother as soon as possible.

"Are you okay?" Kade asked.

"Sure. Who wouldn't be with such a sweet puppy keeping an eye on her?" She glanced at BeeBee still stretched out on her torso and then up at him. A smile claimed her lips as she said, "Hey there."

"Hey yourself." The tension eased from his face as he sat on the edge of her sofa and reached out to scratch BeeBee's ears.

The dog was laying on Iris's chest, completely crashed out. It had been so cozy cuddling with her that Iris was already contemplating how to maneuver more time with his dog. "I think we're going to have to share custody of BeeBee," Iris teased. "I don't think I've had that good of a nap in years."

"I have to admit that I'm a little jealous," he said as he brushed a lock of hair out of her eyes. "BeeBee never cuddles with me like that."

Iris let out a low chuckle. "Oh, and here I was thinking that you might be jealous because she got to cuddle with me."

His eyes twinkled at her. "Why Iris, I do believe you might be flirting with me."

"Am I?" She tried to sit up, but BeeBee stretched her paws out in protest, making her laugh.

"Definitely flirting. And you're not wrong. I'm jealous of both of you. While I was at work, my favorite girl was busy stealing the heart of my pretty neighbor before I even had a chance to compete."

Iris chuckled and couldn't help the grin that spread over her face. Her day had gone from really stressful to this, whatever *this* was. Flirty banter? The start of something more than friendship? Or were they venturing into something closer to hookup territory? The first two options were more than fine with Iris. A hookup, however... She wasn't sure she was built for something like that. She'd never had a one-night-stand or a friends-with-benefits situation. She'd always been a relationship girl, but look at where that had gotten her. Maybe she needed to try something different. Let her hair down. Enjoy herself for once before someone found a way to throw her into jail.

"Why are you looking at me like that?" Kade asked, his voice a little husky.

"I think you know why." She reached up and ran her fingertip lightly over his bottom lip.

Kade sucked in a sharp breath. The sound made BeeBee jerk her head up and look between the two of them with a disgusted expression on her adorable face.

"Stop judging me, BeeBee girl. We haven't done anything," he told his dog.

"Not yet anyway." Iris gave him what she hoped was a sexy half smile as she ran her hand over his muscular forearm. Damn, he was sexy. She'd always had a thing for men who earned their lean muscles through hard work instead of pumping iron at the gym.

"Off BeeBee," he ordered the dog without tearing his gaze away from Iris.

BeeBee opened her jaw wide and let out a loud yawn, making Iris laugh.

"I don't think she's planning on going anywhere," Iris said, amused that his dog had ignored him. Hey, could she blame BeeBee? Their nap had been really comfortable.

"She will," he said firmly, as if he'd already made up his mind on how he was going to get his dog to detach herself from Iris.

"She loves me too much already."

Kade chuckled. "I can't say I blame her." He stood, reached into his pocket, and retrieved a dog treat that looked and smelled an awfully lot like bacon. He walked to the other side of the living room and said, "Come, BeeBee. It's treat time."

The fluffy dog jumped up immediately and ran to her master. She sat patiently at his feet, staring up at him with hearts in her eyes. Iris understood how she felt. It's exactly how she'd felt the moment he woke her up with his gentle touch. Her skin was tingling again just thinking about it.

"Here you go, sweetheart," Kade said to his pup. As she was happily chowing down on the bacon treat, he walked back over to Iris and held out his hand.

Iris took it, and the next thing she knew, she was in his arms, being kissed within an inch of her life.

CHAPTER FIFTEEN

Kade's arms wrapped around Iris, pulling her in close until she was plastered against his long lean body. Her entire body lit up as fireworks went off inside of her. She tilted her head, deepening the kiss, and was rewarded when he let out a low groan.

"Iris," he whispered as he buried one hand in her hair and trailed his lips down her neck, sending shivers through her. "I've wanted you since the moment I first met you."

His words wound through her, making her heart beat faster. How long had it been since she'd felt wanted by anyone, including her ex?

It had been years.

Iris answered him by caressing the back of his neck with her fingertips and arching her neck, giving him better access.

His soft lips covered every inch of her exposed skin, making Iris feel like she was going to melt right there in her living room. Her hands landed on his hips, and without conscious thought, she moved them up under his T-shirt, greedy for his smooth skin and taught muscles.

Gods, she wanted him too. Wanted him more than she'd wanted anyone in a very long time. But even as her body was screaming for her to lead him into her bedroom, her mind was reeling. She'd only known him for two days. And while she liked him and loved his dog, the truth was that she barely knew anything about him. She probably shouldn't be ready to tear his clothes off and have her way with him. Right?

But when his hands found their way under her shirt and trailed up her ribcage, she wanted nothing more than to get naked with this sweet, sexy man.

Iris was almost fifty years old and had never had sex with someone she hadn't been dating for a while. But did that really matter when Kade was making her feel like she was the most desirable woman he'd ever had his hands on?

There was no doubt that she wanted him. Why should she deny herself the pleasure he was silently promising her?

"Iris?" he murmured against her skin.

"Yes?" she answered breathlessly.

"Are you sure you want this?"

There was no hesitation. "Yes."

He let out a growl and then started walking her backward toward her bedroom. Iris tugged his shirt off and nearly stumbled as she stared at his well-defined chest.

Kade chuckled and pressed his palm to her cheek before pulling her back in for another heated kiss. She wasn't even sure how they made it into her bedroom or how he'd gotten her pressed up against the wall without her noticing. The only thing she was focused on were his hands divesting her of her clothes and his gentle touch as he caressed her reverently.

"You're gorgeous, Iris," he whispered as his thumb and forefinger pinched one of her nipples. Pleasure shot straight to her center, making her whimper with the all-consuming need that was clouding her brain. After her divorce, she'd spent entirely too much time standing in front of the mirror while cataloging her body's faults. Her slightly sagging breasts, the stretch marks on her hips, the few age spots that had appeared out of nowhere on her legs.

None of that mattered now. The man cupping her ass and pulling her tightly against him made her feel sexier than ever.

Iris captured his lips with hers and then turned him as she walked him over to her bed. And when she laid down and he was pressing into her, her entire world narrowed to Kade and the pleasure he gave her.

* * *

EVERYTHING about the night before was hot, messy, and perfect. Iris had been completely sated and content when Kade had curled around her as she fell into a deep, dreamless sleep.

"Good morning." Kade's gravelly morning voice made her tingle with the memories of the night before.

Iris rolled over and rested her head on his chest as he tucked her against him with one arm and ran his fingers through her hair. "Morning," she echoed and pressed a kiss to his chest.

Neither of them spoke for a couple of minutes, and Iris was grateful for the comfortable silence. While she liked mornings, it did take a bit for her to ease into them.

A whine came from the side of the bed. Iris peeked over and spotted BeeBee jumping up and pawing at the side of the bed. She chuckled and reached down to haul the sweet girl up onto the bed with them. "Someone was feeling left out."

"Someone is intruding on my one-on-one time with a sexy woman," Kade said as he reached over to scratch BeeBee's ear.

"Aww, give her a break. She slept on the floor all night." Iris laid back down and shook her head when BeeBee crawled right between them.

"See?" he insisted. "Intruder. But you're wrong. She didn't sleep on the floor. When I got up to use your bathroom, I brought her in here and she slept near my feet for most of the night before she got up to get a drink of water."

"She slept on my bed?" Iris asked, surprised. She hadn't even noticed. How was that possible? Usually the slightest noise woke her. Although, she had been physically exhausted when she'd finally fallen asleep.

"Is that a problem?" he asked, suddenly looking concerned as he reached for his dog. "You were sleeping with her on the couch last night, and I just assumed you wouldn't mind."

Iris stopped him before he moved BeeBee from the bed. "Of course, it's fine. I'm the one who just hauled her up here." She gave him a faint smile. "I was just surprised I didn't notice either of you getting up while I was sleeping. I must've been dead to the world."

"You were sleeping pretty soundly." He reached over and brushed a lock of hair out of her eyes.

The tender look he gave her made her heart melt. Holy hell. This man was going to make her fall for him, and she barely knew anything about him other than his name and where he lived and worked. Well, she did know he loved good coffee and dogs. Both of those scored major points in her book. "Kade?"

"Yeah?"

"I don't know that much about you. Don't you think we should get to know each other?"

He chuckled. "I thought that's what we were doing? I don't know if you were paying attention, but I think we learned a lot about each other last night. For instance, I know how you sound when you're turned on and how your breath hitches when I do this." He moved his hand down to cup her breast and lightly pinch her nipple.

Sure enough, Iris's breath hitched as she waited for his next move.

He gave her a self-satisfied smile and flopped onto his back, using that magical hand of his to run his fingers through his hair.

"You're a tease," she accused.

"Maybe, but I'm not getting frisky when my dog is cockblocking me." He stared pointedly at BeeBee, who was still between them.

"Do you think she'd be scandalized?" Iris asked, her lips twitching in amusement.

"Probably." He narrowed his eyes at her. "I suspect that she'd misinterpret what was happening and attack me for hurting you."

That made Iris burst out laughing. "You think?"

He nodded. "There was this one time when I was wrestling with a friend in my living room, and she let out a yelp when I started tickling her. Do you know what this one did?" He pointed at BeeBee.

"She attacked you because tickling is the literal worst?" Iris asked.

"She nipped at me." He shook his head. "She didn't bite, but she certainly let me know whose side she was on."

"Ahh, BeeBee, you're a good dog," Iris cooed and gave her a loving pat.

Kade narrowed his eyes at her this time. "Are you ganging up on me with my dog?"

"Yep." She winked at him and then couldn't help herself

when she asked, "Your friend that you were tickling... Did you date her?"

He shook his head. "Nope, we really were just friends. Good friends though. She moved Back East with her girlfriend last fall."

"I'm sorry," Iris said, imagining that it would be hard to be separated from a good friend like that.

"Sorry that she wasn't interested in dating me? I agree, it was tragic. If only she'd picked me instead of the international model who takes her all over the world on photoshoots. With me, she'd have been able to take walks with BeeBee and maybe get a latte every now and then." His tone was teasing, but she suspected there was something more to what he was saying other than the obvious. He didn't seem the type to care much about a glamorous lifestyle.

Iris thought they were the same that way. All she wanted was a quaint seaside town where people knew and supported each other. It's what she'd found in Premonition Pointe. It's what she craved... community and, if she were honest with herself, a circle of friends like the women of the coven. And maybe a date every now and then with a sexy guy with a sweet dog who adored her.

BeeBee had moved to lying on Iris's chest again and was currently enjoying a shameless belly rub.

"You really liked her, didn't you?" Iris asked.

"Who? Melissa? Oh, no. Not like that." He rolled over on his side and propped his head up on his hand. "Honestly, we were just friends. But I did date someone who I was seriously considering proposing to when she left me for a man with a private jet and three houses. The worst part was that I think she loved me. She just loved his money more."

"Ouch! Seriously?"

He shrugged. "It is what it is."

"I'm sorry," Iris said. "That's really horrible."

He forced a smile. "Not as bad as your husband working for drug dealers and ruining your career."

She winced. "You heard about that, huh?"

"Lucas might have filled me in."

Iris covered her eyes with her forearm. "Yeah, he got involved in moving drugs for reasons I still don't completely understand." She removed her arm and glanced at him. "I guess maybe it was the affair. He started sleeping with the woman who was running drugs, and she sucked him in. Still, we had a good life. Or at least I thought we did. But he ruined it. All of it. Not just our marriage, but the career I worked so hard for, too."

"He's a dick and never deserved you." There was a fierceness in his tone that made her smile.

"Thanks. I agree. Same about your girlfriend who ran off with Mr. Money Bags."

They chuckled together, and when BeeBee whined because she wanted to go out, they both got up. Kade pulled on some clothes while Iris wrapped herself in a bathrobe.

"You take BeeBee out. I'll get the coffee made and start some breakfast," Iris said.

"You want me to stick around for that?" Kade asked. "If you're ready to have your space back, we can head home."

She stared at him, worried that he'd made the suggestion because he was the one ready to leave. Finally, she cleared her throat and said, "You don't have to stay if you don't want to—"

"Oh, I want to," he said as he moved in to wrap his arm around her waist and pull her in close to him the way he had the night before. "If I had my way, I'd spend all day with you.

But I do have to go into work eventually. For now, I'll take coffee and breakfast and maybe watch the sunrise."

Iris beamed at him. "Sounds like a perfect way to start the day."

Twenty minutes later, they were sitting on Iris's back porch with full coffee mugs and bagels and cream cheese with BeeBee running around the yard.

"I think your dog is in love with my flowers," Iris said, amused that BeeBee kept sniffing her lavender garden. "It's sweet how she's careful not to trample anything."

"She does like her flowers. I bet she'd move in here if I gave her the choice. Naps with you and lavender? What more could she need?"

"Her daddy," Iris said automatically. "Every girl needs her daddy." Why had she said that? Her heart ached the way it always did when thoughts of her own father crept in out of nowhere.

"Iris?" he asked, reaching over and covering her hand with his. "Are you all right?"

She let out a humorless laugh. "I sound that pathetic, huh?"

"No. Just sad all of a sudden. Is it about your father?" There was concern in his eyes, and while she never talked about her father to anyone, she felt compelled to share what happened that terrible day. It was a pain she hadn't shared with anyone before, but for some reason, she wanted to tell Kade.

Trust, she thought. That was it. Deep inside, she instinctively trusted him. That was enough.

"I lost my father when I was six years old. He was taking me to get ice cream at the corner market. My mom was mad about something. They'd been fighting, and I was crying because Dad had promised to take me ice skating. At that age, I was determined to be a princess on ice." Iris's eyes watered as she chuckled. "If you saw me skate, you'd know I was delusional."

He smiled softly at her. "I'm sure you're good at anything you put your mind to."

"You're sweet but very wrong. I have weak ankles and skated like it. My mom always feared I'd break one just by trying to stand in the skates. She was exaggerating of course, but they were always sore after I wobbled around the ice for a couple of hours."

"I still say you would've grown into it." He winked. "Go on. What happened to your dad?"

Iris swallowed hard. "Like I said, he and Mom were fighting. It was a screaming match. She was insisting he quit his job, and he kept refusing, saying that he needed to make enough money to fund all of her projects first. I didn't understand what he meant at the time, but knowing what I know about her now, he was right to not quit his job."

This time when she paused, Kade stayed silent, waiting for her to continue.

When her heart stopped racing, she said, "He stormed out of the house, and I ran after him. He seemed startled to see I was there at his side, but he just took my hand, smiled down at me, and insisted we go get ice cream." Iris sucked in a deep breath before she started speaking again. "It was a gorgeous summer day. Blue skies. Birds chirping high overhead. But it didn't last. Not long after he bought our Drumsticks, something caught his attention across the street. His eyes narrowed, and he muttered something about work always interfering. Then he cursed, gave me a little shove, and ordered me to go home. He said he'd be along in a few minutes."

"Did you?"

Iris nodded. "He said it in his dad voice. There was no

disobeying, so I started to head home. But then he cried out for me to run. There was panic in his voice. I'll never forget it. I was scared, so I took off."

Kade reached over and placed his hand over hers, waiting for her to continue.

"I hadn't gotten more than half a block when I heard the gun go off." Iris sucked in a fortifying breath, willing herself to get this out. "When I turned around, Dad was on the ground, unmoving. I didn't understand what had happened at first, but then people started screaming and scrambling around. One woman stopped to try to help Dad. She pressed her own shirt to his chest wound. All I remember was dropping my Drumstick and running back to him. When the ambulance came, they had to pry me off of him to get him onto the gurney. I had blood all over my white T-shirt and jeans. I must've looked like I was the one who'd been shot. It was horrific on every level."

They were quiet for a long moment. Iris wiped tears from her eyes and continued to focus on BeeBee so she didn't have to see the image of her dad in her mind.

Finally, Kade squeezed her hand and asked, "Did you ever find out who did it?"

The raw pain that always filled her when she thought of that day almost overwhelmed her, but Kade's hand holding hers grounded her. For the first time in memory, she didn't feel like she was going to vomit while remembering that day. "No. Mom said they called it a random act of violence, but I never believed it." She turned to meet his eyes. "He saw someone he knew before he ordered me to leave. To this day, I'm convinced that his death was premeditated murder. But back then, no one would listen to a six-year-old. And when I bring it up with my mom, she always shuts down the conversation. She says that's in the past and there's no reason to open old wounds."

Kade nodded. "I can see why she takes that position. I'm sure it's still painful for her, too."

"I guess so," Iris said even as frustration seized her. "The problem is that I don't think either of us ever really dealt with it. I've always wanted to find out more about that day, to find out what happened to my dad. But she's locked everything about him away as if he's some sort of dirty secret never to be spoken about again."

"Come here," he said as he got to his feet and tugged her up into his arms.

Iris went willingly. His strong arms wrapped around her, making her feel safe. It was a strange feeling for her. No man since her dad, not even Tom, had ever made her feel protected. She relaxed into him, grateful just to be there.

"If you haven't already, maybe you should talk to someone about your loss," he said, stroking her hair.

"You mean like a psychologist?" she asked.

"Yes. It might help."

She couldn't deny that she'd thought about it before. But her mother hadn't thought it necessary, and Tom had said it would hurt her career if anyone found out she was seeking therapy. She wasn't so sure about that, but the discouragement had been enough to keep her from making an appointment. "You're probably right," she conceded. "It might be time."

BeeBee came running up right then, jumping on Iris's leg. She bent down and picked up the pup, needing the distraction. She was petting her and telling her what a pretty girl she was when Kade said, "I went to therapy after my mom passed away. It helped."

Iris turned to him. "What happened to her?"

"Overdose. She'd been in a car accident and got addicted to pain pills." He was focusing on BeeBee as he added, "I was nine."

"Oh, Kade. I'm so sorry," Iris said, her heart breaking for him. "I can't imagine."

"Can't you though?" He met her gaze, his deep blue eyes emoting an ocean of pain. "You saw your father gunned down in front of you. What I went through wasn't all that different. It was the catalyst for a contentious relationship with my father, especially after he married my stepmother less than a year after my mother's death. It's the reason I worked so hard to get that scholarship to the boarding school Back East. Getting out of that house was the only way I survived my teenage years, and that seemed like a better plan than running away."

Iris stared at him, recognizing that he was telling her they had a lot more in common than she'd realized. Knowing how much she hated talking about the trauma of her past, she didn't say anything. Instead, she stepped into his personal space, wrapped her arms around him, and held on tight. "Thank you," she whispered.

"For what?" he asked.

"Just being you."

He let out a breath, tightened his hold on her, and said, "You're welcome."

CHAPTER SIXTEEN

*A*ll too soon, Kade was standing at Iris's front door, kissing her goodbye. It had been one hell of a night and morning. She'd shared more of herself with him than she'd ever thought possible. Twenty-four hours ago, all she'd known about him was that he had a sweet dog and was a nice guy she wanted to get to know better.

Now, she felt a deep connection to him both mentally and physically. Frankly, it scared the hell out of her and even though she didn't want him to leave, she knew she needed the time apart to collect her thoughts.

"Are you free for dinner?" Kade asked when he finally let her go and took a step back.

Was she free? Probably. Should she have dinner with him or give herself more time to process whatever was happening between them? Before she could even answer her own question, she nodded. "What time?"

"Around seven? I could cook something for you, or if you prefer, we could go out somewhere." He stared down at her lips, looking like he was going to kiss her again.

"Stop that." She swatted at him playfully. "Save that for later after you feed me."

"So my place then?" he asked, his lips twitching into a smile.

"Definitely." She pressed up onto her tiptoes and gave him the kiss he was obviously craving. When he finally let her go, she was breathless and a little dazed as she watched him and BeeBee make their way to his house.

Iris closed the door softly and then leaned against it, taking a moment to collect herself. It was a good thing her mother wasn't an early riser. If she'd run into Kade, no doubt she'd have given him the third degree and embarrassed the hell out of Iris. Tact wasn't a trait her mother possessed. And that would've definitely ruined the perfect evening and morning she'd shared with Kade. "Damn," she whispered, knowing that if she wasn't careful, she was going to fall for him. Hard.

Was that a bad thing?

The question ran through her mind, both thrilling her and freaking her out. She was not in a place in her life where she was ready for a relationship. It was time to get to work on clearing her name. She would not be going down for the curse someone else had inflicted on the town that she loved.

IRIS PULLED her car to a stop in front of a small cottage that was in an older neighborhood on the other side of town. Most of the yards were well maintained, but there were a few that were unkempt and in need of city citations for cleanup. One was clearly a fire hazard with too much dead brush, and the other had broken-down, rusted cars in the yard which wasn't allowed in residential neighborhoods. She made a note to call them in and then cursed herself.

What was she doing? It wasn't her job to deal with city matters anymore. But she couldn't help herself. She'd call them in and get someone to write a letter letting the residents know they had to clean it up or the city would do it for them and send them a bill.

After double-checking Julie's address, Iris killed her car engine and hurried across the street to her former assistant's home. She'd never been there before, but was grateful she'd had her address in her phone. She still had the addresses of everyone who'd worked with her because she'd sent them Christmas and birthday cards.

The front door was open, leaving only the screen as a barrier to the house. Iris rang the doorbell and refrained from peeking through the screen as she waited.

"Iris!" Julie gasped out, immediately opening the door and yanking her former boss inside. "You shouldn't be out there."

"Why?" Iris asked, confused. "I heard you were fired from the mayor's office. What else can they do to you if they see us talking?"

"You don't understand." Julie paced her tiny living room. It was decorated with all white furniture and had brightly colored paintings on the walls. It was tasteful and happy in a way that was one hundred percent Julie. "I've been instructed not to talk to you. If they find out..." She trailed off as she wrapped her arms around herself and shuddered.

"Who threatened you?" Iris asked, her body vibrating with anger. What in the hell was going on at the city offices, and why had Iris been so careless as to bring Julie into it?

"Tad did when he fired me. He said if I talked to you about anything concerning the mayor's office, he'd have me arrested for obstruction and fined for... Hell, I don't even know what for. I was stunned by the whole thing and terrified they were going to frame me for something just like they did you." Her voice broke on the word *you*, and tears streamed down her face.

"Julie," Iris said softly and moved to wrap her arms around her former coworker. "I'm so sorry I got you into this mess. If I hadn't called you for information, this never would've happened."

"Yes, it would've," she said with a sniff and stepped back, dislodging herself from the hug. "I've known from the very beginning that you'd never curse Premonition Pointe, so I was snooping around the office, trying to find evidence to clear your name."

A surge of hope burst through Iris. "Did you find anything?"

Julie let out an exaggerated sigh and slumped down onto her overstuffed couch. "No. Not about the curse, anyway. Still, Tad caught me going through his file cabinet. I told him I was looking for paperwork that a business owner submitted for a plan to expand their parking lot, but when he asked for details, I didn't have them. I told him that's why I was looking for the paperwork. He didn't believe me, obviously. Then at the end of the day, he fired me." She grimaced. "That's when he told me he knew I was loyal to you and that if I helped you in any way, I'd live to regret it."

Iris shook her head. "He's a giant dick."

"You're telling me." She wiped at her teary eyes and said, "But before I got booted, I did find out who typed that message for the thousand-dollar assessment you asked me about. His name is Dylan Michaels, and he's been an intern since the day after you left."

"Dylan Michaels?" Iris frowned. Why did that name sound

so familiar? She knew that name; she just didn't know from where. "What does Dylan look like?"

"Redhead with lots of freckles and really long—"

"Eyelashes," Iris finished for her.

"You know him?"

"He used to work for Tom at the lumber mill before Tom was forced to sell it." The lumber mill had been her ex-husband's business when they were married. It was where he helped distribute drugs for the woman he'd been sleeping with. Part of the deal to not prosecute him had involved him selling the business.

"Really? That's... a huge coincidence," Julie said, rubbing her forehead as if she were trying to make sense of it.

Iris disagreed. It wasn't a coincidence at all. There was no doubt in her mind that Tom had gotten him the job with the new mayor. It made her wonder if Tom was actively involved in getting her ousted from her position. Just the thought of that pissed her off. If he had been, she was going to make him wish he'd never met her, let alone married her. "It's suspicious at best," Iris said. "But this is really helpful, Julie. Thank you."

"You're welcome. I just wish there was more I could do." Her eyes filled with tears and she tried to blink them back. "I'm sorry. I just... I don't know what I'm going to do now that I've lost that job."

Iris pulled her into a hug. "You'll find something. And if you don't, let me know. I'll help you. Even though I'm going through it right now, too, I still have connections."

Julie hugged her back, and her body shook with tears as she gasped out, "Thank you."

"No thanks necessary," Iris said, meaning it. Julie had been a great assistant. She didn't deserve the treatment she'd gotten from Tad. As Iris held on to the other woman while she tried to get herself under control, a very vivid image of Julie flashed in her mind. The woman was standing on the bluff high above the sea where the coven met each month. She was alone with the wind in her hair and golden magic illuminating her hands as she chanted something Iris couldn't make out. Suddenly, a bolt of magic came down and connected with the sea, sending Julie flying. She landed on her back, staring up at the sky. A moment passed, and a slow smile claimed her lips.

The image vanished, and Iris jerked away from Julie. She opened her mouth to ask her about it, but Julie stiffened and said in a low voice, "You have to go. Through the back door."

"Why?" Iris asked, glancing around and seeing nothing alarming.

"The Magical Task Force agent just pulled up outside. If she sees you here, she'll have to report it, and then who knows what will happen?" Julie started pushing Iris toward the kitchen and the back door.

Iris glanced back at the front door, and sure enough, she spotted a glimpse of the MTF agent she'd spoken to the day before. "Dammit, Tad," she muttered, furious that the little maggot had any control at all over what she did or didn't do. But she couldn't risk putting Julie in the path of his wrath again.

"Iris!" Julie hissed. "Please."

"I'm going," she said quickly. "But remember to call me if you need anything, all right?"

"I will." She hurried over, opened the back door, and ushered Iris out.

Iris snuck around the side of the house and waited until Julie invited Ginny Stevens inside before hurrying over to her car and taking off like she was some sort of wanted criminal. The entire encounter made her feel a little sick to her stomach. She shouldn't have to be sneaking around to visit Julie. The moment Iris got her hands on Tad, he was going to wish he'd never messed with her. She'd make sure of it.

CHAPTER SEVENTEEN

*I*ris desperately wanted to head straight for Dylan Michaels' house. She just might have, too, if she'd had any idea where the kid lived. She'd tried to log into the city records again, but they'd finally changed the password.

"Kid," she scoffed. As if a twenty-something was still a kid. He was old enough to know right from wrong. Maybe he didn't understand that the memo he'd written was illegal without a town vote, but Iris had a hard time believing that the young man who'd worked for her husband and who was now Tad's lackey didn't have a clue that his bosses played dirty. She was certain he was in on whatever scam the mayor and city council were running.

She could call Tom and ask him where Dylan lived, but then she'd have to explain why she wanted to talk to him and that was a conversation they were never going to have. She didn't trust Tom anymore. There was no way to know how much of what she said to him would get straight back to the new mayor. No, she'd have to find Dylan's address another way. She pulled over into a gas station and killed the engine.

Surely Google would tell her where he lived. But before she could type in her search, Gigi's name flashed on the screen of her phone.

Some of Iris's anxiety fled when she saw her new friend was calling. "Hey, Gigi. What's up?"

"Where are you?" Gigi asked.

"In my car. Why?"

"Because Skyler and I are standing on your porch and you aren't here," Gigi said, her voice sounding urgent. "Skyler has news. Big news from the gayssips. We need to talk..." Gigi's voice was muffled when she spoke again, as if she'd lowered the phone from her mouth. "Oh, hi there. Are you looking for Iris?"

"No. I'm her mother," Katheryn said in an icy tone, her voice coming through the phone crystal clear. "Now, if you'll step aside, I'd like to get into my house."

Her house? Iris thought immediately, then forced herself to put that minor detail out of her mind. She had bigger things to deal with.

"My mother is there?" Iris asked, frowning. Whatever Skyler wanted to tell her, she didn't want him doing it in front of her mom. Katheryn would just lecture them about letting the lawyers handle everything. There was no way she had confidence that Iris could help herself.

"She just got here," Gigi said. "Do you want Skyler to tell her what he found out?"

"No!" Iris shouted into the phone.

"Okay. Ouch. What was that for?" Gigi asked, clearly confused by Iris's outburst.

"Sorry," Iris said, trying to force herself to calm down. Her mother's reappearance, at exactly the wrong time as usual, sent her blood pressure skyrocketing. Man, if she'd ever needed an anti-anxiety pill, it was at that moment. "Do not tell her anything. It won't go the way any of us hope it might. Can we meet somewhere else?"

"Hold on." Gigi spoke in a muffled voice again, and when she came back on the line, she said, "How about Skyler's boutique? He has some orders to get ready for shipping, and that way he can multitask."

"It works for me. I'll bring the coffee," Iris said. "If I'm getting dirt on my arch nemesis, then I'm gonna need some java to pick me up. Give me your orders and I'll be there in twenty."

Gigi rattled off a couple of complicated drinks that Iris hoped she wouldn't mess up, and then ended the call just as Katheryn was demanding to know what they were still doing on her porch.

Some things never changed. Iris's mother was always going to be an overbearing presence in her life. At least she took comfort in knowing that her mother didn't only behave that way around her daughter. It appeared to be a universal thing with her.

Iris made it to the café and then to Skyler's shop in sixteen minutes flat. She was rather pleased with herself, knowing that she was on time and had the one thing she truly needed in life to carry on—her afternoon latte. After downing that, she'd be ready for anything.

Or so she hoped, anyway.

When Skyler and Gigi arrived at his storefront, Skyler immediately grabbed the cup that had his triple-shot espresso latte with extra cream and a dash of cinnamon and handed Gigi her nonfat, sugar-free, vanilla iced latte. He took a long swig, let out a satisfied grunt of approval, and then unlocked the door for them.

"Gods, I hate that you had to shut down while this is happening," Iris said.

"Me, too." Skyler ran a hand through his blond hair and scanned the showroom that was devoid of any customers. "It feels like a mannequin is going to come to life at any moment." He glanced around, a panicked look on his face. "Does this mean I'm going to turn into Andrew McCarthy?"

Iris couldn't help it. She laughed. "How do you even remember that movie? Aren't you a little young for that?"

Skyler shrugged. "Pete likes all the eighties classics. If a romantic comedy from that time exists, I've likely seen it."

"So have I," Gigi said. "And I have to say that I really don't think you have what it takes to be Jonathon in *Mannequin*. You'd freak out the moment she got on the back of your bike and pressed her female boobs against your back."

"Ugh, I would, wouldn't I?" He frowned. "Way to ruin my gay fantasies. I was hoping I'd get a male mannequin, but now that you've brought up other options, maybe it's not worth risking it. Besides..." Skyler glanced at the only male mannequin he had in the showroom and said, "His package probably wouldn't be that impressive would it?"

Iris glanced over at the mannequin in question and chuckled. "Not impressive at all. Better stick to the real thing, Sky."

He shrugged. "Sure. Pete's the only man I want or need anyway. Especially after what we learned today. I'm going to hole up all week and make Pete... um, well, spend quality time with me. Sounds fun, right?"

"Sure," Iris agreed, crossing her arms over her chest. "Now, why don't you tell me what you learned about Tad? I'm dying to know the gayssip."

Skyler laughed and covered his mouth. "Sorry," he said

between two fingers. "I'm just not used to you using the word *gayssip*. But believe me when I say the tea they spilt, girl, it's a doozy."

"Okay. Lay it on me," Iris said, braced for the worst.

Skyler squared his shoulders and blurted, "Tad is part of the same drug ring your husband was involved with. They're in this together."

"Mayor Tad is involved in that drug ring?" Iris cried and then fisted her hands in her hair as she added, "And my ex is *still* involved?" That would explain why Tom had tried to get her to leave town. He knew that if she got wind drugs were circulating again that she'd do everything in her power to stop it. But why did they curse the town? That seemed really bad for business. Although, ever since the leader, Yasmeen, had gone to jail earlier that year, she hadn't heard of any more drug issues in Premonition Pointe.

"That's the rumor," Skyler said. "A friend of mine knows a guy who knows a guy who was hired to build out a warehouse about thirty miles east of here to process Ashe."

"Well, that would make a certain amount of sense since Tom's lumber mill where they were processing it was shut down when it was sold." Iris sank down onto a settee near the register. "What else did this friend of yours know? And how accurate do you think his information is?"

Skyler pursed his lips together, appearing to consider her question. Then he sighed. "Probably not one hundred percent, but I bet there's a lot of truth to it. This friend, while he's sober now, used to be into the drug scene when he was younger. He still knows people who know stuff. He runs private fishing tours and relies on tourists for business. He's not at all happy about what's going on, so he's been asking questions."

Iris nodded. "I can imagine. Does he have any more

information that might be useful? Like the exact location of this warehouse?"

Skyler leaned against the counter and took a long sip of his coffee before answering. "Sorry, he doesn't know where it is. His contact wasn't willing to say anything about that other than it was deep in the woods."

"That's too bad. It would've been satisfying to send the DEA out there on a raid." That was definitely something Iris would love to see.

"It would, but there's something that might prove to be even more useful," Skyler said with a gleam in his eye.

"Uh-oh, this is getting good," Gigi said as she moved to sit next to Iris and wrap an arm around her shoulders. They both stared up at Skyler, waiting for him to continue.

"So the warehouse," Skyler said and nodded to Iris. "Your ex, Tom Hartsen, apparently helped them set it up. He was paid big money and told to get you out of town or else they'll throw him under the bus the next time they get caught. This operation is being run by some people who are in law enforcement. So that tells us why he got off without serving any jailtime when he was caught red-handed."

Iris scowled. "I'd wondered about that, but we didn't have any proof that Yasmeen had anyone on the inside. Do you know who they are? The DA maybe?"

"I don't," Skyler said, shaking his head. "Whoever the higher-ups are, they are staying in the shadows. It actually sounds like they are floating names of their minions so that they are the face of the corruption if anything hits the fan."

"Minions?" Gigi asked. "Who else are they talking about."

Skyler's smile turned wicked. "Tad. The new mayor. He was offered the position if he became one of their drug mules."

Iris blinked. "Tad is the drug mule? How exactly is he doing that?"

"According to my source, a small amount of a very pure form of Ashe is being smuggled through the pharmacy. Tad picks it up with a bogus prescription for anxiety and then mails it out to a high-profile customer. It brings in a lot of money. Enough to make it worth his while to get rid of a certain former mayor."

Iris let out a gasp. "The other day Kade and I tailed Tad to see what he was up to. It seemed very boring at the time, but do you know what he did?"

They both shook their heads.

"He went to the pharmacy and then straight to the post office." Her heart raced, knowing that this was more than just a rumor. "I think your information is likely on target, Skyler."

"I hope not," he said, frowning. "I sure don't want them to be successful in getting rid of the former mayor."

Iris grunted, knowing he was talking about her. "They can try, but I'm not easy to erase."

"No doubt," Gigi said, her expression stormy. "We need to do something about this. The coven can help root out the bad actors."

"But how?" Iris asked. "We can't curse them, and until we know who we can trust in law enforcement, it's risky turning them over to the authorities. Look at how well that turned out where my ex was concerned. A slap on the wrist and he's right back in the middle of things."

"We need to talk to Sebastian," Gigi said. "He'll be able to find someone who's trustworthy, even if he has to look for someone out of town who works with the state instead of the local law."

"That's a good idea." Iris peered at Skyler. "Any other

rumors?"

"Just that the cartel that we're dealing with here excels at blackmail, so there's a strong possibility that most of the ones involved, like Tad or Tom, are being blackmailed to do their bidding."

"That's what Tom claimed when he was dragged down last time," Iris said. "Since he'd never broken the law before that, I was inclined to believe him. But now? He could've asked law enforcement for help, since he turned state's evidence in order to avoid jailtime."

"Not if this runs deep in the department," Gigi said. "What if it was all for show last time? Do we know for sure that Yasmeen went to prison? Maybe that was all smoke and mirrors to make us all think it was over."

"Think about it," Skyler added. "If they kept Ashe off the streets and distributed it elsewhere, no one would suspect that the people involved hadn't actually paid the price for all those overdoses that happened here in town."

Iris's stomach churned. Young people had died on her watch from overdosing on that horrible drug. She'd thought she'd done the work to eradicate it from Premonition Pointe, but if what Skyler was saying had any truth, all that had happened was that the cartel managed to get her fired and had gone right back into business without her even noticing. The very idea made her want to vomit. "We need to stop them."

"We need to talk to Sebastian," Gigi said again. "See what he suggests so that you don't get into even more legal trouble."

"How would I do that?" Iris frowned at her friend.

"Oh, I don't know. By doing something stupid like intercepting those packages Mayor Tad sends out?"

Iris raised one eyebrow. "That's not the worst idea."

Gigi stood and shook her head. "Yes, it is. Interfering with mail is a felony. You're already in enough legal trouble."

"So you're saying we need to tip someone off at the post office to check those boxes?" Iris reasoned.

"Maybe," Gigi said and then nodded. "Yes, that could work. I like it. It's unlikely the postmaster is involved in any of this, and that would be one way to make sure this doesn't get swept under the rug."

"It's a plan," Iris said. "We'll still talk to Sebastian, but the next time we spot Mayor Tad going from the pharmacy to the post office, I'll make the call."

"No. I will get Sebastian to do it," Gigi insisted. "It's better if it doesn't come from you. The conflict of interest might make them not take you seriously."

"I like it." Skyler clasped his hands together. "Can I go on the stakeout with the sexy lawyer? That would be hot."

"I'm telling Pete you're perving on my man again," Gigi said with a sigh.

Skyler chuckled. "Oh, honey. You talk as if Sebastian isn't already the star of Pete's jerk-off sessions."

"Skyler!" Gigi threw a throw pillow at his head. "Don't ever say something like that to me again. I do not need to know anything about what gets you two off. Just… no. Let's stick to vintage clothes and face cleansers from now on. Got it?"

Skyler snickered, and despite the upsetting news that Ashe was at the center of all her problems, Iris felt herself smile. There were still a lot of questions to work through, and she was far from out of the woods with her legal issues, but at least she felt like they had a plan forward. As long as she stayed focused on the problem, she was certain that with the coven's help, they'd have Premonition Pointe cleaned up and back to normal in no time.

She just wondered who she could trust in the meantime.

CHAPTER EIGHTEEN

*I*ris felt unsettled, like she needed to do something to relieve the nervous tension that was making her jittery. The afternoon with Skyler and Gigi had been productive. There was no question that she'd been framed. Someone else had cast that curse, and they were pinning it on her in order to get her out of town. They just needed to prove it. How, she wasn't sure. But at least they had a plan to get to the bottom of the corruption in Premonition Pointe. If they caught Mayor Tad in the act of distributing Ashe, that would go a long way toward forcing an investigation.

The issue for Iris was that she was used to being in charge. She wanted to go full steam ahead and start investigating everyone from Tad to the AG to every last police officer on the town's force. Unfortunately, Gigi had been right. Sebastian had forbidden her from getting her hands dirty in any of it. He'd said he'd put his team on it and let her know what they found.

Sitting on the sidelines wasn't Iris's strong suit, so when she walked into her house that evening, she was already testy. The moment she walked in, she grimaced when the overwhelming scent of cedar assaulted her senses.

"Mom!" she called out, making a beeline for her kitchen. Cedar meant one thing; her mother was making a potion. But what kind of potion and why? Her mother's cedar potions were usually really powerful magic, and Iris just didn't want her doing anything that could bring suspicion down on them. There were already too many questions she couldn't answer. "What are you doing?"

"Making a potion. What does it look like I'm doing?" she asked. Katheryn was wearing faded jeans and an old sage green T-shirt under Iris's favorite checked apron, and her hair was up in a careful bun so that nothing was likely to contaminate her concoction.

"Obviously it's a potion," Iris said, fully annoyed. "What kind of potion and why? Right now, we should be laying low, not using our magic. I don't need you causing me to be accused of any other nefarious deeds. And yet, here you are, making one of your famous potions. Can't you see that's a bad idea?"

"It's not a bad idea," she said haughtily. "In fact, it's the best idea I've had all month, and eventually you'll thank me for it."

"Thank you for it? When do you think that will be?" Iris challenged. All her frustration had bubbled to the surface, and Iris was unable to hold anything back. "When the Magical Task Force agent shows up again and accuses me of spelling someone because they accidentally drank a potion that you made?"

Her mother stopped what she was doing and turned around to look her daughter in the eye. "Doesn't that sound just a little hysterical to you? Why would anyone else be drinking a potion I'm making for you?"

"I don't know." Iris threw her hands up. "Why did you cleanse the magic from the backyard? Now I have the MTF agent writing a report that indicates I might be trying to hide something. Sebastian got the charges dropped, but right after the agent picked up on that epic blunder, she told me not to be surprised if they use that to build a tighter case. In other words, I could be hauled off to jail because of something you did." There'd been a lot of vitriol in Iris's tone, but in that moment, she didn't really care. Her mother needed to back off and stop trying to fix things. She was only making them worse.

"I didn't do a cleansing spell in the backyard. What makes you think that?" her mother asked. Her brow was furrowed, and she looked genuinely confused.

Iris wasn't buying it. "It was the day you cleaned the house and started ordering me around about how I should be living my life. Agent Stevens from the Magical Task Force was here and said someone had swept the backyard of magic. It certainly wasn't me. I wouldn't even know how to do that. But you... You definitely have both the skills and the knowledge to get that done, and while I'm sure you think you were just helping me, you need to just own up to it, Mother. Otherwise, I could be forced to deal with the consequences."

"I didn't—" Katheryn started.

"Stop lying! Look at you. You're making a potion right now," Iris yelled. The tension from the past days of living with her mother just came out all at once with zero regard for trying to keep the peace. Iris was done with other people trying to run her life. Completely done. Her mother just happened to be the first one in her crosshairs. "I just can't trust you, Mom. I think it's time for you to leave." She crossed her arms over her chest, determined to hold her ground.

Katheryn's eyes narrowed, and her face flushed red as she scowled at Iris. "You're throwing your own mother out?"

"I just think it's better if we have some space from each other. Don't you?"

Her mother turned around and took a moment to pour the potion into a glass bottle. After capping it, she pushed it to the back of the counter, ripped her apron off, and tossed the pot she'd been using into the sink, causing everything to clatter so loud it hurt Iris's ears.

Iris just watched her, wondering when the outburst would come. Because there was no doubt it would. As much as Iris hated to admit it, she'd gotten her short fuse from her mother. Once they were pushed to the breaking point, neither of them had ever been able to hold back.

Katheryn finally turned to Iris, and in a terse voice, she said, "If you don't want my help, then fine. I'll go and leave you to it. However, don't forget that everything I've done here this week has been to help you."

"Help?" Iris repeated. And even though she knew she should've kept her mouth shut, there was no stopping her now. "I think you might be overstating things, Mom."

Katheryn threw her hands up. "Fine. I'll go." Her eyes blazed with fury, but her tone was even when she spoke again. "Do us both a favor and don't toss the potion out. You're going to need it when Tom and his new *friends* decide they are done with you." Katheryn swept past her daughter, leaving her eyeing the dark green potion that was still on her counter.

What in the world was she talking about? She stared down the hall after her mother. It wasn't long before Katheryn reemerged with a designer suitcase and her purse. That wasn't all of her luggage, but she supposed her mother was making a grand exit. After Iris's outburst, who could blame her?

"What does that mean? That I'm going to need the potion when Tom decides he's done with me?" Iris asked, all of the anger she'd been feeling under wraps. As frustrating as her mother could be, there was no denying that she was a skilled witch. One of her skills was the power of sight. She sometimes saw visions and other times just knew when something was going to happen. Had she had a vision of Iris?

Her mother sucked in a deep breath and let it out before speaking. "Tom is going to find a way to poison you. That potion will save your life. So keep it with you at all times. Do you understand?"

Iris gaped at her.

After a few seconds, Katheryn snapped her fingers in front of Iris's face. "Iris? Did you hear me? They will try to kill you. I've seen it happen half a dozen ways. That means there's no changing it. The only thing to do is prepare. Got it?"

Iris nodded, her entire body numb. "Tom is going to try to kill me?"

Her mother nodded. "It won't be by choice, but he'll do it anyway to save his own ass. I always did think he was a coward."

She hadn't been wrong. If only Iris had paid attention to her mother's opinion, she might not have wasted all those years with Tom when she could have been with someone like Kade.

Kade?

Where had that come from?

Katheryn strode over to the door, glanced back, and said, "You can call me when you're ready to apologize."

Iris opened her mouth to protest but then shut it and just watched her mother walk out. If her mother was right, and

Tom did try to poison her, Iris would owe Katheryn much more than an apology.

Still, it was a good thing her mother was leaving. They both needed their space. Or was that something Iris was just telling herself to feel better? She didn't know, and honestly, what did it matter at that point? All she could do was try to relax and get some rest. She was going to need it.

CHAPTER NINETEEN

Iris was just getting out of the shower when there was a knock at her door. She hurried through the house in her robe and let out a curse when she checked the time. It was seven o'clock, and she was running late for her date with Kade.

Assuming the person on the other side of her door was Kade, she pulled the door open and stammered, "Sorry, it's been a long day. I— Tom? What the hell are you doing here?"

Her ex pushed his way in without waiting for an invitation.

Iris immediately thought of the potion on her kitchen counter and kicked herself for not asking her mother for details. How long did she have to drink the potion before she lost all control of her body if Tom really did poison her? How much did she need to drink? Did the potion expire? Surely it was still good only a few hours after it had been made, right?

"We need to talk," Tom said, spinning and placing his hands on his hips.

"No, we don't. You need to get the hell out of my house,"

she demanded as she pointed to the still open door. "No one invited you in."

"I used to own this house," he practically snarled at her. "Now you're telling me I need permission just to enter the living room?"

"Yes!" Iris barked out, clutching her robe tightly to her body. "That's exactly what it means when one party buys the other one out in a divorce. This house doesn't belong to you anymore. And neither do I." She jerked her head toward the door. "Now I have to ask you to go. I have plans and I need to get dressed."

He scanned his gaze over her, his eyes lingering on her chest where the robe was trying to gap open. "Yes, you better do that before your date gets here and gets an eyeful of more than he bargained for."

Iris was ready to scratch his eyes out. She hated that she didn't know if his statement was a jab or some sort of weird compliment. Iris glared right back and ordered, "Just say whatever it is you came to say, Tom."

"Maybe I just came by to see how you're doing. Did that ever occur to you?" He straightened his shoulders and stared past her as he added, "I always did tell you the mayor's job was more trouble than it's worth. Honestly, you're lucky you got to quit."

"I didn't quit," she said, eyeing him like he'd lost his damned mind. "I was forced out, thanks to you."

"Hey, let's not lay blame at anyone's feet," he said more amicably as he shoved his hands in his pockets and rocked back on his heels.

"You're a real piece of work." She shook her head and held the door open. "Go, before I call the police and have you hauled out."

A predatory smile claimed his lips. "You can try that, but I doubt it'll work. No one is going to believe that I broke in here. And even if they did, there's video proof that you let me in when you opened the door... in your robe no less."

"Video proof?" she gasped out. "Where exactly? Because we already got rid of the nanny cams that were in this house. You wouldn't know anything about those, would you?"

He gave her a bored look and shrugged. "Nanny cams? I don't know what you're talking about. I was referring to the neighbor's door cams. I'm sure we can get footage if we need it."

His reaction was more than enough to convince her that he had been the one to plant those cameras. Otherwise, he'd have been at least a little surprised that someone had been watching her.

How had she ever been married to this man? The only thing she felt for him now was disgust. Where was the sweet man who'd brought her flowers for no reason and was always ready for a walk down to the beach? The one who cooked for her and told her how much he loved being married to a strong woman. It was all bullshit. She knew that now. He hadn't been able to handle her being successful and had found someone else who made him feel important. It had cost him everything. Their marriage. His business. The town's respect. And even his shame apparently, because in that moment, he had none.

Tom sat on the arm of her sofa and eyed her thoughtfully.

"What?" She glanced at the clock and gritted her teeth. No doubt Kade was wondering where she was.

"You need to let this thing with the curse go, Iris. Let the new mayor handle it. He knows what he's doing. Not every problem needs your hands in the pie, you know?"

"I'm not letting go of anything," she said, raising both

eyebrows at him. "Do you really expect me to ignore a curse put on Premonition Pointe? You, of all people, know how much I love this town. I can't just watch the businesses suffer. We have to fix it before their bills come due. No customers. No money."

"They'll be taken care of," he insisted, sounding irritated. "But if you keep persisting, then I can't say what might happen."

"Is that a threat, Tom?" she asked, this time her voice hard as steel.

He took a step back and mumbled something about wanting her to be safe.

Sure he did. Was that why he was going to try to poison her?

"Iris, just listen to me. The people who did this— They don't like you."

"I know," Iris said, completely comfortable with that fact. She didn't care for them much either.

"Something terrible will happen if you don't do what they say, and I just couldn't live with myself if I wasn't around to stop it," Tom continued.

"What exactly do you want me to do, Tom? Move away?" Iris asked. "Leave Premonition Pointe to the wolves and see who survives after a territorial fight?" She'd started off glib, but now she was just exhausted by all the mind games. "You know what? Never mind. I'm not going anywhere. This is my town, not yours. You don't even live here anymore."

"I only live thirty miles south of town," he said as if that made a difference to her.

"So? This isn't a competition. I've already said I'm not leaving, so stop wasting your breath," she said icily.

Tom let out a growl of frustration before stalking to the

door. He turned back, his gaze both frustrated and sad. "You're going to regret this moment. Mark my words."

Iris shook her head. "The only thing I'll regret is letting you back in the door." Iris stalked over to him and gave him a shove right out the door and onto the porch. "Now go home, Tom, before that poison burns a hole in your pocket."

She couldn't help laughing at Tom's shocked expression. He appeared to be completely stunned by her outburst. Good. Now he understood that she knew about the poison. If that wasn't enough to stop him, nothing could. She made a point of glancing at the potion Katheryn had left on the counter again, just in case she needed it that night.

"Iris, you need to see reason," Tom started.

"She needs to get over to my house." Kade's voice came from the porch steps, just behind Tom. "It's almost time for dinner."

"I'm sorry," Iris said, meaning it more than ever. She hated that Kade had found her in her terrycloth robe, hair up, and no makeup. That right there was enough for a jury not to convict her for killing Tom when she murdered him.

"No need to apologize," Kade said. "But let me know if you need help getting rid of the ex. I'm happy to call security in."

"We have security?" she asked, already fantasizing about Tom being hauled off by burly security professionals.

"We do."

Tom put his hands up in the air as if someone was trying to rob him and shook his head. "No. Don't call security. I'm going. I was just trying to warn Iris that she'll be better off if she stops worrying about the town curse."

"We all know that's not going to happen, so I think your time here is up," Kade said. Then he looked at Iris. "Is that right?"

"Hell yes," she said as she pulled Kade in, glared at Tom, and then slammed the door shut, leaving her ex on the porch to wonder what she and Kade had going on. She hoped he was imagining the dirtiest thing possible.

With that on her mind, she turned to Kade and said, "I'm not really hungry. Not for food anyway. How about we skip dinner and just head straight for bed?"

He grinned at her. "I like the way you think. Lead the way."

CHAPTER TWENTY

"Good morning." Kade's gravelly voice woke Iris from her contented sleep.

She pried her eyes open and yawned in the darkness. "It's not even daylight yet."

He wrapped his arm around her and pulled her in close so that she was lying on his bare chest. "If we're going to make it to our sunrise hike, I figured I'd better wake you up."

"Right." But a hike wasn't what Iris had in mind. Not yet anyway. The night before, right after he'd helped her kick Tom out of her house, they'd stormed into her bedroom and the fireworks had gone off. Their lovemaking had been hot and frantic and needy. Hands and mouths were everywhere, and they hadn't slowed down until they were both breathless and completely spent.

It had been the hottest night of her life. Images of slick bodies and echoes of the sounds they'd made had her skin tingling again. In her nearly fifty years on Earth, she'd never been so turned on by anyone.

"How much time do we have?" she asked before trailing kisses along his neck.

Kade let out a small groan of pleasure and rolled them over so that he was hovering above her. "Enough for this." He covered her mouth with his as she wrapped her arms and legs around him and once again was lost in everything Kade.

* * *

BY THE TIME Kade and Iris made it to the end of the trail where the redwoods opened up to a dramatic canyon, the sun was already high in the sky. A silver river cut through the valley below them and still churned with the year's snowmelt from the nearby mountains.

"We missed it," Kade said, leaning against a sign that marked the historical significance of the area. "I really wanted to show you the sun coming up over the mountain range."

"You showed me something else quite spectacular this morning." She winked at him, feeling more relaxed and happier than she had in months. It wasn't just the sex either. It was the quiet time they shared hiking through the woods together. The moss and redwood scents that mixed in the fresh air. It made her wonder why she didn't take time to explore the woods more often.

Kade chuckled. "Well, when you put it that way." He took a step forward and lowered himself onto a large boulder. "Come sit with me."

Iris went gladly and snuggled into his side, enjoying being enveloped in his warmth. "Thank you. This might be the most perfect first date I've ever had."

"Would you really call it a first date?" he asked, his tone teasing.

"First *formal* date, then." She gazed out at the mountains in the distance and let out a sigh. "You know, I always gravitate toward the ocean, but this is really soothing, too. I can't believe we're lucky enough to live in such a gorgeous place."

"It's easy to take for granted when we're caught up in life stuff," he said. "Want to make a pact to get out on the trails once a week?"

The offer both lit her up with excitement and made her heart sink. It sounded so wonderful to have a hiking partner with the promise of spending a lot more time just enjoying the wonders that nature had to offer. But then the doubts crept in. What if Tom and his band of criminals really did manage to frame her for the curse on Premonition Pointe? Would she be spending her mornings behind bars, just thankful that she got to see the sun at all? The thought made her shudder, and she briefly wondered if she should leave town after all. It wasn't as if she had deep roots keeping her there. Her only living relative was her mother, and she had a house in Las Vegas. Who else was left? Gigi and Skyler and the coven. And of course, now Kade. But they'd only been in her life for a short time. Was it worth it to stay and risk her freedom?

The answer was swift and resolute.

Iris wasn't going anywhere.

She loved her town. There was no question about that. But it was more than that. She felt like she'd finally gotten to a place in her life where she was making important connections with the coven and now Kade. She knew deep in her soul that there was no way she was giving that up due to horrible people who belonged in jail.

"Iris?" Kade asked. "We don't have to go every week if that's too much. How about a hike once a month? That might be easier to fit into your schedule."

"No," she said, shaking her head.

"Oh. All right." He frowned as he stared past her.

"No, that's not what I meant," she tried again with a nervous laugh. "Sorry. I meant no to the monthly hike. I like the weekly idea." She gave him a shy smile. "I was just thinking about everything that is going on and wondering if I'd even be here for those hikes. With the way that things are going, I just… It's hard to make plans."

"Maybe making plans is exactly the right thing to do," he said, taking her hand in his. "You need to have something to look forward to after all of this is over."

Iris leaned her head on his shoulder and sighed. "Gods, that's a nice thought. That at some point this will all be over. I thought I was going to get to move on after my divorce, and then all of this happened. How was I supposed to anticipate any of this?"

Kade pressed his lips to her head, giving her a kiss. "No one could anticipate that the town would be cursed or that someone would try to frame you. You can't predict bad actors, because they do things that would never even occur to you."

"That's… true. I don't have a devious mind," she said, shaking her head.

"You've got a good heart, Iris Hartsen," Kade said. "It's what attracts me to you most."

She turned and smiled up at him. "So do you. Though your protective nature is pretty attractive, too."

He chuckled and tightened his hold on her. The silence that fell between them was comfortable in a way that Iris hadn't experienced with another man before. It made her want to know more about him, and before she could think better of it, she asked, "Have you ever been married before?"

"Nope. Not even close," he said. "Was Tom your only marriage?"

She nodded and grimaced. "I always told myself I was only ever going to get married once. Divorce isn't something I ever saw myself doing. And the sad thing is that even though I know now that our marriage was just a shell of a relationship, if Tom hadn't cheated or gotten involved in a drug ring, I probably would still be married to him even if it meant ignoring the fact that I wasn't happy."

He turned to meet her gaze, and she quickly turned away, not wanting him to see the pain that had to be written all over her face. "Iris, look at me."

She closed her eyes but then forced herself to do as he asked.

Once he was holding her gaze, he asked, "Why? You're clearly a strong, independent woman. This isn't a judgment, but I don't understand staying with someone who doesn't add to your life. What made you hang in there?"

"My mother," she said. "After watching the wreckage of her life after my father was killed, I always said I'd never go through that. She was married five times in eight years. The irony is that the one person she truly loved, my father, she never actually married."

"Your mother was married five times in eight years?" Kade asked. "You can't be serious."

"Oh, I'm quite serious. Four of them were clear mistakes," Iris said. "I always thought the serial marriages were because she was trying to recreate what she had with my dad and thought that was the way to do it. Or maybe she was just trying to mask the pain. Whatever the reason, clearly, she wasn't ready for something new. Though her fifth husband, Warren, I thought that he might last. He was sweet to both of us. There was never any drama, and they seemed happy. But then one day he packed up and left. My mother never would say what happened. She just said something about some people not being meant for marriage. At the time, I thought she meant him, but now I think she was talking about herself. She hasn't been with anyone seriously since then. I was sixteen when he left."

Kade kneaded the base of her neck. "It makes a lot of sense now that you were willing to fight so hard for your marriage. You wanted a different pattern for your life. That's admirable."

"Is it though?" She tsked and shook her head. "I didn't fight for Tom. I just ignored what was happening. The truth is, I cared more about my job than him or our life together. What does that say about me?"

"That you had a shitty marriage, and because of past trauma, you were doing what you thought you should do to protect yourself from more pain?"

Iris felt tears burn her eyes. She let herself flop backward until she was lying on the earth, staring up at the blue California sky. "I should never have married him."

"Maybe," Kade said, staring down at her with a thoughtful expression. "Or maybe you were supposed to in order to understand what you want, and don't want, for the rest of your life. Surely there must've been some good times together. It wasn't all bad, was it?"

"No. We were good friends before he went sideways," she conceded. "I just..." She was about to say that after a few nights with Kade, that she now knew she'd been living a life without color. One where she walked in shadows instead of sunlight. But that was way too cheesy. Or at least way too soon in their love affair. If that's even what it was. She hoped so, but whatever this was, it was too new to be putting any kind of label on it.

"Just what?" he prompted.

"I know now that I legally tied myself to someone that I wasn't passionate about. I won't do that again. Ever."

He brushed his thumb over her cheekbone and whispered, "Good."

She stared up at him, admiring his strong jaw and kind eyes. "What about you? You said you'd never even come close to marrying before. But was there anyone that you thought might be the one?"

He shook his head. "I dated. Had a couple of long-term girlfriends, but I always knew I wouldn't marry them. One stayed longer than she should have because she needed a friend. We were close in college. The other one, she was just there for the money."

"Money?" Iris raised one eyebrow. "Weren't you a scholarship kid?"

He chuckled. "Yep. But I started a tech company with a friend of mine and not long after we graduated, we sold it. We didn't make fuck-you money. It's not like I'll be buying a yacht anytime soon. But it's enough that as long as I'm careful, I can basically do whatever I want to without worrying much about it."

"That's great, Kade. Good for you." Iris pushed herself back up into a sitting position. "I wish I could say the same. Unfortunately, having to split assets with the ex means my resources were drained. So I'll need to get a new job soon. I just wish I knew what I wanted to do."

"You don't have any idea?" he asked, checking his watch and then getting to his feet.

"I think I'd be a great business consultant, but I'm not sure demand around here is high enough for that. Besides, I don't have any formal training. I don't know who'd hire me without that on my résumé."

Kade held his hand out to her and helped her up. "I think just about any business owner in Premonition Pointe would hire you."

"Why do you say that?" she asked, narrowing her eyes at him.

"Lucas and I talk at work. I know you've helped a bunch of them find ways to be profitable. And you're forever promoting them, too. They'd be fools to not hire you."

"Maybe. But if they all think I cursed the town, that's not gonna win anyone over." She shoved her hands into the pockets of her jeans and desperately wished her nightmare would end.

"Sebastian's not going to let them pin this on you, and eventually the truth will come out. It always does," he said, placing his hand on the small of her back and leading her back toward the path.

Iris appreciated him for trying to be supportive, but they both knew there weren't any guarantees. Anything could happen with the investigation. She just prayed she came out of it with her freedom and a modicum of respect from the residents of Premonition Pointe.

"You know what my dream job would be?" Iris said just to take her mind off the case.

"What's that?"

"Angel investor. You know, like the investors on *Shark Tank*. I'd be really good at that. My single biggest strength is knowing when an idea is going to take off."

"Yeah? Give me an example."

Iris followed him into the canopy of redwoods and started

rattling off the ideas she'd encouraged that had taken off. "It was my idea for Skyler to open a high-end vintage clothing section in his shop. He was just intending to sell his original designs, but I mentioned that our tourists, who tend to have a little more money, would love access to designer clothes. And that it would probably help his bottom line, since the retail space he wants is so big."

"That is a good idea. Lucas says we have a lot of folks asking for modern era furniture at the shop. We're going to start making some in that style, but he mentioned picking some up at estate sales to see how they do."

Iris let out a cry of happiness. "Good. I'm glad he's doing that. It will be the perfect complement to his business."

"What else has your genius mind come up with?" Kade asked as they started to descend into the woods.

"Nothing really special. Just things like knowing if another candy store will thrive, or if Premonition Pointe is ready for a vegan restaurant, or if a ghost tour would be popular versus a celebrity tour. I just seem to have a knack for knowing right away if it's the right thing for our town. I used to think of it as my one magical gift, only now we know there's more power in these old limbs that I never even knew about."

"You know, that is one hell of a handy skill to have," Kade said. "I'll keep that in mind in case I ever decide to start another business."

As they made their way back down the trail, they spent the rest of the morning throwing out ideas for the most ridiculous businesses they could think of. Things like actual dental floss bikinis, an ebook bookstore, and custom snowshoes in a town where it never snowed. But when Kade tossed out an idea for pet weddings, Iris let out a loud laugh and said, "Hope already arranged a dog wedding. It's not as bad an idea as you think."

He groaned. "That's next level crazy."

"Maybe, but she made a nice paycheck that day."

Iris's limbs were pleasantly fatigued when they finally reached the trailhead. The fog had started to roll in, and it was hard to see where they'd parked Kade's car. "I think it's this way," Iris said, already moving in the direction she'd indicated.

"What the—" There was a muffled groan, followed by the scuffing sounds of someone fighting to stay on their feet.

"Kade?" Iris turned around, frantically looking for him in the fog that was getting denser by the second.

He didn't answer.

"Kade!" she called again just as a black SUV sped past her, kicking up dirt and gravel and forcing her to close her eyes against the debris.

The car made a squealing noise as it turned out of the small parking lot, leaving Iris alone with no Kade, no keys, and no idea what had just happened.

CHAPTER TWENTY-ONE

*P*anic took over. Iris's entire body trembled with fear as she ran after the SUV, only to be met with a deserted road and fog so dense she could barely see ten feet in front of her.

"Shit!" she cried and reached for her phone that she thankfully had tucked in her back pocket. After frantically moving her fingers over the phone, she managed to make a call to Sebastian.

It went straight to voicemail.

"Dammit!"

Gigi was next with the same result.

Tears of pure frustration stung her eyes. She searched her phone and came up with Grace's number.

"Hey, Iris," Grace said, her voice breathless. "Can I call you back? I was just about to—"

"No! Kade was just abducted, and I'm stranded out here at the Whistler Point trailhead. I don't know what to do." Her stomach cramped with stress, and she had to bend over to suck in air.

"Kade was abducted? What do you mean?" Grace asked, sounding just as stunned as Iris felt.

"I mean, we came off the trail into some thick fog, and he was taken by someone in a black SUV. I didn't see anything but the car speeding away. We need to do something."

"Did you call the police?" Grace asked.

It was a reasonable question. Any sane person would've done that first, but Iris hadn't even considered it. Her trust in Premonition Pointe's government officials was too broken. "No, I... I don't know who to trust."

"Right," Grace said, her voice now full of resolve. "Someone will be right out to get you. Don't worry. We'll find Kade."

"Grace?" Iris said before she could hang up.

"Yes?"

"Thank you."

"There's nothing to thank me for. Hold tight."

IRIS WAS PACING the parking lot when a black truck jerked to a stop beside her. She peered in and found Lucas King reaching to open the door for her.

"You okay?" he asked as soon as she climbed in.

"No. Not at all. One minute he was here, and the next he was gone. I have no idea where to start looking for him."

Lucas slammed his foot on the pedal, and they sped onto the two-lane highway. "Hope and Grace are already assembling the coven. I'm to take you to the cliff so they can do a finding spell. Do you have anything of Kade's that you can use to connect to him?"

Iris considered the question. Kade had been at her house the night before. Maybe something was there? If not, maybe she could get into his house. "Not with me. Can you take me home? I think I might be able to find something."

"Sure thing." Lucas reached over and squeezed her hand, giving her the support she didn't even know she'd needed.

While she'd been waiting for one of her friends to pick her up, she'd gone numb inside. While she'd found something in Kade and the coven that was miraculous, her life and everything she'd built had fallen apart. How was this all going to end, and was there any way she'd survive it? It was hard to imagine in that moment.

"It's going to work out, Iris," Lucas said as if he'd just read her mind. "I know everything is fucked right now, but your girls won't stop until they've found him."

Iris squeezed her eyes shut and let her head rest against the cool window. "Gods, I hope so."

When they pulled up to her house, Iris's eyes went wide with surprise when she spotted BeeBee sitting on her porch at the front door. As soon as Iris jumped out of the truck, BeeBee darted toward her and pressed her small body against her legs. "What are you doing, sweetheart? How did you escape your house again?"

The dog whined and stared up at Iris with sad eyes. "You know he's missing, don't you? Well, don't worry. We're going to get him back." Instead of entering her own house, she went to Kade's and tried the door. It was locked. She glanced down at BeeBee. "How did you get out?"

BeeBee barked once and then ran around the side of the house to the back. She slipped through a small section of the gate that had rotted away and barked again. Iris reached up and unlatched the gate. Once she was through, she spotted the open back door. "So you busted out the back, huh? All right.

Let's get something of your dad's, lock up, and get moving. We have a finding spell to cast."

Ten minutes later, Iris, BeeBee, and Lucas hiked through the fog and found the coven already setting up around the stone firepit.

"Iris!" Gigi ran over and engulfed her in a tight hug. "I'm so sorry neither of us answered your call. Sebastian was headed to the office, and I was busy working on a new potion."

"It's okay." Iris hugged her back, grateful for the support. "I got hold of Grace, and she put all of this in motion." When Iris let go of her friend, she took stock of the witches gathered around the circle. Grace, Hope, Joy, and even Carly Preston, the famous actress that had moved to Premonition Pointe the year before. "Uh, hi."

Hope moved forward and took Iris by the arm. "Come on. We're almost ready to start. Did you bring something of Kade's?"

Iris produced the sweatshirt he'd been wearing the day before. "Will this do?"

"Should be fine," Grace said, taking the garment from her and placing it on a stone in the middle of the circle.

Carly Preston moved to stand next to Iris and leaned over to whisper, "I hope you don't mind that I'm here. I'm sure you heard about when my niece went missing."

Iris nodded, not sure what that had to do with Kade's abduction.

"I just know how traumatic this is for you because I've been there. When Joy said my magic would be useful, I didn't hesitate. But I wanted to be sure you're okay with this."

"Of course," Iris said, letting out a breath. "Thank you. I'll take all the help I can get."

Carly placed a soothing hand on her arm. "If anyone can

find him, it's this coven."

Iris nodded, believing her. The women in this coven had proven to be a force to be reckoned with. It's why she went to them the moment Premonition Pointe was cursed. Hopefully they'd have better luck at finding Kade than they had figuring out who cursed the town so far.

"Lucas?" Iris asked. "Can you watch BeeBee and make sure she doesn't get into the circle?"

"Yep." He took BeeBee's leash and moved off to the side, giving the coven the space they needed.

"Who's leading this?" Joy asked.

Everyone turned and looked at Iris.

"Me? But I barely know what I'm doing!" she cried.

"You have the strongest connection to Kade," Gigi said. "It's better if the spell comes from you."

"But I have no idea what to do." Iris stared at the candles already lit and illuminating the circle and then turned her attention to Kade's sweatshirt. Her insides were churning, and there was a hole in her heart that made her feel as if her time with Kade was over. Even if they did save him, would he really want to be mixed up with someone who got him abducted because... She had no idea why they'd taken him. She assumed it was to force her to fall in line with what they wanted.

"I'll lead you," Gigi said. "The flower petals have already been crushed. All you need to do is chant the spell and sprinkle the flower petals on the sweatshirt."

"Flower petals?" Iris asked.

"They're from his yard," Gigi explained. "They'll help with the connection."

Iris took a deep breath and let it out. "That seems reasonable. Okay, let's get started."

"Just do what I do and repeat what I say," Gigi said.

Iris watched her friend intently and copied her when she raised her arms high in the air and then repeated her words. "Goddess of the Earth, we seek one of the heart. Show him to us before he is lost."

The candles flickered and the wind picked up, howling in Iris's ears. But she barely noticed. All she was thinking about was that Kade was the one of her heart. She hadn't bothered to question Gigi on the wording of the spell. Iris knew it was true, and if that connection helped, then she was all in.

"Toss the flower petals in the circle," Gigi ordered.

Iris did as she was told and chanted the incantation again. The other witches echoed her chant, and together they all raised their faces to the foggy sky and demanded the earth goddess show them her child.

Magic crackled through the air, making Iris's skin prickle with energy. She focused harder, imagining Kade's face, his smile, his gorgeous eyes, and finally his warm heart. Her own heart started to race, and she felt as if she was lifting right out of her body, staring down at the circle, watching as the magic warred with the air. Shapes formed and dissipated only to repeat the pattern over and over again.

"You need to try again!" Gigi ordered. "Picture Kade. See what he looks like, and feel what he feels like, and smell what he smells like."

Iris did exactly that. She pictured him sitting at the summit of that trail, smiling softly at her as they admired the view. Then her mind shifted to the night before and the way her skin had tingled as he touched her all over. The scent was harder. He wore some sort of aftershave, but that wasn't the scent she wanted to recall. It was the earthy wood smell of him after he'd spent all day working with Lucas.

As soon as her senses conjured up the sweet, woodsy smell

of redwood, the circle brightened with a flash of light, but the person who appeared hovering over the sweatshirt and flower particles wasn't Kade.

It was her mother, Katheryn.

"Mom?" Iris gasped out. "What—"

"Listen, baby. It's important. Understand?" Katheryn said, her eyes filled with pain and regret.

"I'm listening." Iris had no idea what was happening. Maybe the spell failed. Or perhaps her mother had hijacked it. Iris didn't know, but her mother was hovering in the circle. Her perfectly tailored suit was askew and torn in places as if she'd fought a battle and lost.

"They've got me. After all these years, they finally got me. If you want to save me and Kade, you need to find Warren. He'll know what to do."

"Warren? Your ex-husband?" Iris asked, confused. They hadn't heard from him since she was sixteen years old.

"Yes. Warren. He'll know where we are. Hurry, honey. They've been waiting for me a long time."

The image started to fade, making Iris panic.

"Mom! Wait! Where do I find him?"

"His cabin," she managed just before the image winked out.

The wind stopped and the candles blew out suddenly, leaving the entire coven standing on the fogged-in bluff staring at Iris.

Iris dropped her hands to her sides and squatted down, needing a moment to collect herself. What in the world did Warren have to do with any of this? And where was his cabin?

Gigi cleared her throat. "It looks like we have to find someone. And sooner rather than later."

Iris nodded, turned around, took BeeBee's leash from Lucas, and walked as if in a trance up the hill toward her house a few blocks in from the beach, trying to process what had just happened.

She'd tried to summon the man she was falling in love with and instead ended up with her mother, who delivered a semi-cryptic message.

Though if Warren really did know where to find them, then that meant... son of a bitch! Was everyone who'd ever been in her life corrupt?

She looked around at the coven members and knew that wasn't true. She also didn't believe it about Kade. But then again, why had they taken him if he wasn't shady?

To get to her, obviously. If anyone had been paying one iota of attention to her, they'd have realized that even though she'd only known him for a few short days, she was still falling head over heels for him.

"Iris?" someone said from behind her.

She spun, ready to go off on whoever had followed her. Couldn't a girl get even a few moments of peace when she was trying to process something as traumatic as realizing that both her mother and her new boyfriend had been abducted.

"What is it?" she barked, unable to hold in her emotions. Then she mumbled an apology when she spotted Ginny Stevens, the young Magical Task Force agent who was standing a few feet away.

"Oh, hell," she sighed. "I'm sorry. I really don't have time for this. I've already told you everything I know."

"While that might be a bit of an overstatement," Ginny said with a laugh, "I do believe that you had nothing to do with the curse, and I thought you'd like to know that Internal Affairs has been called in. Mayor Howell is officially under investigation. The charges against you have been dropped, permanently."

CHAPTER TWENTY-TWO

*W*hen Kade's cottage came into view, Iris's chest tightened. Too much had happened, and she was having trouble processing.

The news that she was no longer a suspect for the curse still plaguing Premonition Pointe was welcome, but she certainly didn't feel the relief or vindication she knew she should, because the people who mattered most had been taken from her.

Kade, the man she was starting to need more than she cared to admit, and her mother, who, no matter how overbearing or frustrating, was the one person who'd always been a constant in her life. Iris was willing to do just about anything to get them back.

With BeeBee by her side, Iris ran into her house and immediately went to the guest room to see if her mother had left anything behind before she'd stormed out the day before. The bed was unmade, and there was a pile of clothes in the corner that she must've missed when packing her bag. But there didn't seem to be anything that had any sort of information on Warren's cabin.

She searched through the dresser and the closet and even the spare bathroom, as if she was going to find a journal or the address written in lipstick on the mirror or something equally as ridiculous.

It was no surprise when she came up empty-handed.

"Dammit, Mother!" she cried in frustration. "Where am I supposed to find this information?"

"Iris?" Grace said, appearing in the hallway.

"Yeah?"

"Come here." She held her hand out, inviting Iris to take it.

Iris stared at her friend's hand, and instead of screaming in frustration, she took it and let the other woman lead her into her living room.

"Here." Grace handed her a bottle of water. "Drink this."

Iris glanced around her living room, finding the entire coven hanging back, waiting until they were needed.

"We've got you," Grace said, putting an arm around her and leading her to the couch. "You do realize that we're here to help you find Kade and your mother, right? It's not you against the world. Every single one of us has your back."

Hope, who was nearest, nodded. Joy was perched on a chair opposite them, typing away on a computer. And Gigi and Carly were having a heated debate on whether another finding spell would work.

"I don't have anything of Warren's," Iris said. "I haven't even seen him in over thirty years."

"Do you have a picture of him?" Carly asked.

Joy's head snapped up. "I didn't even think of that."

The two shared a glance, and Iris wondered what was happening there. She cleared her throat. "I might. Let me go check." She took off for her bedroom with BeeBee close behind. After rummaging in her closet for a shoebox full of photos she'd had since she was a teenager, she gathered BeeBee and the pair sat down on the bed. BeeBee curled up on her pillow while Iris lifted the lid off the childhood memories that she hadn't ever wanted to revisit but hadn't been able to toss out either.

The photos on top were of her high school graduation. The smiling girl staring back at her appeared happy on the surface, but Iris remembered that day all too well. Her mother hadn't come home the night before, and Iris had woken to an empty fridge and a note from her mother that said she'd be out of town for three days. There was a twenty stuffed under the keys to the old barely reliable VW Bug that her mom had gotten her for her sixteenth birthday.

Iris hadn't even been surprised. That was the saddest part of it all.

She'd sucked down instant coffee, spent twenty minutes trying to get the VW to start, and then walked to the bus stop. The only reason she'd made her graduation on time was because a neighbor whose grandson was in her class stopped and gave her a ride. The picture in the box was taken by the photographer that snapped each student's photo as they walked across the stage. Iris had purchased it with her own money and promptly threw it in the box where she'd never looked at it again.

Iris sighed and started sifting through the photos. There were a few that were good memories. The ones from camp, where she'd spent two weeks every summer for three years when she was a preteen. There were ones when she was little before her dad passed. Her favorite was one of them together as he showed her how to bait a hook. She was staring at him with a look of adoration. In the next one, she was holding a small fishing pole with a tiny fish and had a huge grin on her face.

A small stab of pain hit her right in the chest. What would her life had been like if her father hadn't been killed? She closed her eyes and took a moment to remember the man who'd loved her so completely.

A cool nose nudged her hand, and when Iris looked down, BeeBee was there, pressing her head against Iris's leg. "Thanks, baby girl. I needed that."

She quickly went through the rest of the pictures, pausing briefly to take in one of her and her parents that had to have been taken right before they lost her father. He had his arm around her mother, and Iris was standing in front of them with an ice cream cone, her smile wide. They looked so happy.

A flashback of her mother tucking her in that night and then reading with her until she went to sleep flashed in her mind. Iris frowned, trying to remember if that had been a normal evening. Something told her it was. She had memories of her mother snuggling her and them giggling under the covers. But that had all stopped when her dad died. Her younger self had ached for the mother she'd known then, only to be left with one who had fallen apart and never quite figured out how to put herself together. Not until Warren came into her life anyway.

Dammit, she needed to find Warren as soon as possible. She tossed the pictures from memory lane aside and dug deeper until she finally found one of herself and Warren. They were standing in front of the VW Bug, laughing at something.

"Hopefully this will do," Iris said and stuffed the rest of the pictures back into the box. With BeeBee tucked under one arm and the pictured clutched in her hand, she hurried back out into her living room where her friends were huddled together discussing a spell. "I have one."

Joy rose from her spot on the couch and moved to her side. She held her hand out. "Do you mind?"

"Not at all." Iris handed it over.

"Anything, Joy?" Carly asked.

Joy slowly nodded. "I think so."

Iris glanced between the two of them. "What are you talking about?"

Carly placed a hand on Iris's arm. "Joy can sometimes see visions if she has a photo of someone. It looks like she might be able to tap into where Warren is. But it will be easier if the coven works together to enhance her magic."

All the members of the coven had already gotten to their feet.

"Okay, where are we doing this?" Iris asked, anxious to get started.

"Outside," Carly said and took Iris by the hand. The star held on tight and led Iris to the backyard. When they were on the deck, Carly turned to her. "Are you doing all right?"

Iris shrugged one shoulder.

Carly rubbed her palm down Iris's arm. "I get it. I've been there. Just know that if you need anything, a shoulder, an ear, private detectives, I'm here, willing, and able."

Dammit. Tears stung Iris's eyes again. "Thank you."

"No need, but you're welcome." Carly pressed a sachet of herbs into Iris's palm. "These are for protection."

Iris stared down at the small bag.

"Keep them in your pocket, just in case."

"I don't—" Iris started.

"Trust me," Carly said. "The people who took Kade and your mother likely did it to get to you now that you're no longer a suspect in the cursing case. The Magical Task Force is looking at the mayor and who knows who else. We don't know what they'll be willing to do next, but it seems likely it's something to frame you again. Or blackmail you into taking the fall. It's best to be prepared."

She definitely had a point, and Iris took it to heart. Nodding, Iris shoved the sachet into her pocket and turned to the others who had already gathered around her. "What do we do next?"

"Form a circle," Grace said. The normally stylish realtor was dressed in faded jeans and an old faded T-shirt. Her long auburn hair was tied up in a messy bun and she looked like she hadn't made any plans on leaving her house that day. The other members of the coven were in similar states of dress, each of them looking like they'd bolted from their houses the moment they got the call that Iris needed help.

"Thank you," Iris said with a rush of gratitude. "For being here. For helping me with no questions asked."

"That's what covens do," Grace said. The others nodded their agreement.

"But I'm not in your coven," Iris said. "I just appreciate—"

"Yes, you are," Hope said. Her dark eyes were narrowed as she studied Iris. "At least you are if you want to be."

"She's right," Grace said.

"Yep. We don't turn away sisters." Joy smiled at her. Then she turned to Gigi and Carly. "Right, ladies?"

"Right," Gigi said.

Carly nodded. "I think we've all reached a point in our lives that when we find someone we connect with and trust, we don't let them go. I know that's how I ended up a part of this group."

"Amen," Gigi said.

Joy smiled at them and then turned to Iris. "They're right. We feel a connection to you, so you're one of us as long as you want to be."

Do not cry, Iris ordered herself. There was no time for that. But the unexpected support from the group of women surrounding her was overwhelming, and one lone tear ran down her cheek. "Thank you," she managed to squeak out. "I'm honored to be part of your coven."

"Perfect," Grace said. "Now let's get this spell started. We have people to find. Iris, please stand in the middle of the circle and hold up the picture of Warren."

Iris did as she was told, and after the candles were lit, the rest of the witches started chanting. "Goddess of the earth, show us the path we seek."

They chanted the phrase over and over until eventually the air turned chilled and the scenery blurred. Magic coated her skin, but it wasn't heavy. She felt as if she were floating through space and time with her toes hovering just above the ground.

When she blinked, her vision cleared, and she was standing at a crossroads. The predominant street sign read *Upper Valley Hwy* while the one that pointed down a dirt path read *Five Point Crossings.* Iris took a step down the dirt road, but as soon as her foot hit the ground the wind picked up and lifted her back into the air. She was thrown backward as her world turned black. When she blinked again, she was standing in the circle in her backyard with her coven around her.

"Holy shit. That was… strange," Iris said.

"What did you see?" Joy asked.

Iris described the road and the signs to them.

Joy nodded. "I saw a cabin on a dirt road. It had a five-point star on the door. If we can figure out where Upper Valley Hwy is, I think we can find Warren.

"I'm on it," Hope said, already tapping away at her phone. It was only a few seconds later when she threw her hand in the air in triumph. "It's a couple of hours east of here. Who's up for a road trip?"

CHAPTER TWENTY-THREE

"*I* hope the entourage doesn't scare him off," Gigi said as she glanced behind her at the car following them.

"I doubt it. Warren isn't the type to scare easily. Or at least he wasn't." She prayed that was the truth. When they'd been deciding who would go along with Iris, no one from the coven was willing to stay behind just in case there was trouble. She was just glad that none of their partners had demanded to come along. Otherwise, they'd have needed to rent a bus.

"Sebastian is working on a background check," Gigi said as she tapped away at her phone. "He says he can't find anything on Warren since he was married to your mom."

"That's not unusual, right?" Iris asked. "It just means no arrest records or bankruptcies. That sort of thing?"

"No... I mean, yes, but he hasn't found anything at all. No credit. No major purchases. No businesses in his name or where he's listed as an employee. It's like he's in the wind. Very strange. Usually his background checks bring in something interesting."

Iris glanced over at her and ignored the queasy feeling in

her gut. "That doesn't necessarily mean anything." Though she knew that wasn't true. If nothing was coming up, it meant that Warren was intentionally keeping himself below the radar.

Gigi raised an eyebrow at her. "I've looked for people before. That's not normal."

"Ugh. I was trying to lie to myself," Iris admitted. "I don't think I can handle one more person going off the rails."

"I'm not sure you have a choice, but at least your girls will have your back." Gigi tucked a strand of her blond hair behind her ear and lowered her sunglasses. "I think the turn is the next left."

Iris's gut churned with nerves, but she tightened her fists on the wheel, determined to see this through no matter what she found at the end of that dirt road. The sign at the intersection was the exact same one she saw in her vision, making her certain she was on the right path. She turned down the dirt road and felt her pulse pick up as they rolled past a thick line of trees and overgrown scrubs.

"Joy says the cabin is just ahead," Gigi said, looking up from her phone.

Iris nodded, and when she rounded a bend in the road, a one-story cabin with a metal roof came into view. There was an old wooden swing on the weathered front porch and a five-point star on the door.

Joy's vision had been spot-on, making it clear they'd found the right place. But even if that hadn't been the case, she'd have known this was the spot by the old blue '58 Chevy pickup with the dent in the tailgate. Her breath caught as she remembered the day she'd dented the pristine vintage truck when she'd backed into it with her VW Bug. Why hadn't he ever fixed it? Warren's hobby had been restoring vehicles. The repair would've taken him just a few days at most.

She pulled the car to a stop behind the truck and immediately jumped out. Now that she was there, she couldn't wait to talk to Warren. She knew her mother sent her there for a reason, but now she just wanted to wrap her arms around the only stepfather she'd loved and pray that he hugged her back.

Before she could even knock, the door swung open.

"What do you want?" Warren's voice was gruff and menacing, and if she hadn't known him, she likely would've run back to the car, cowering in fear.

But she did know him. She'd witnessed those narrowed eyes and his scowl before. Underneath the growly man used to be a softy who'd do anything for her. She took in his silver hair and the same green eyes that were now surrounded by deep wrinkles. He'd aged, but he was still handsome in a Harrison Ford kind of way. "Hi, Warren. It's been far too long."

It took a minute, but his scowl vanished and his eyes widened as he swept his gaze over her. "Holy shit. Iris?"

She grinned at him. "I bet you didn't think I'd find you way out here."

He let out a surprised chuckle. "No. As a matter of fact I didn't. How did you find me? Katheryn?"

Iris nodded and her grin vanished. "Mom's been abducted. She sent me to you. She said you'd know what to do."

Warren's brow furrowed. "What do you mean she's been abducted? What happened?"

"I don't know why they have her, but I can explain everything else that's happening," she said.

He opened his door wide and invited her in.

Iris stepped through the threshold and was surprised to find a cozy home with comfortable-looking furniture and pictures lining the wall. She couldn't help herself when she went straight for them, only to be shocked when she found they were all of her and her mother and one she never expected. Iris turned to him, her hands shaking as she asked, "You knew my father?"

He nodded slowly and walked over to the framed photo.

The two men were young, probably in their early twenties. They each had an arm draped over each other's shoulders, and they were grinning like fools. Iris pressed her fingertips to the glass and then looked at Warren. "How did you know him?"

He cleared his throat. "Nate and I sort of grew up together. Ran with the same crowd after high school."

"You're kidding," she gasped out. "Does mom know?"

Warren nodded. "Come into the kitchen. I'll get you something to drink while you fill me in and explain who's waiting for you outside."

"Gigi is in my car. The one behind it is full of the rest of my coven members. If I don't text them to assure them you haven't locked me in your basement in the next two minutes, they'll likely break your door down and curse you at first sight."

"You're part of a coven?" His eyebrows rose practically to his hairline.

"Hey!" she cried. "Don't act so surprised. Jeezus."

He chuckled. "Sorry. I just seemed to recall your mom trying to teach you magic and that it never went very well."

Iris flopped down into one of his chairs at the breakfast table. "That's right. I seem to have come into my power just recently. The badass women of Premonition Pointe seem to have welcomed me into their fold."

"That's good. You deserve to have people like that in your life." He pulled a pitcher out of his refrigerator and grabbed two glasses. After filling them with lemonade, he sat next to her and reached out to place his hand over hers. "It's really good to see you, Iris."

"I wish it was under better circumstances," she said and turned her hand so that she could squeeze his.

He nodded in agreement. "Tell me what's going on and how I can help."

"Like I said, I don't know why Mom was taken." She told him the entire story about how she was the former mayor, how the town had been cursed and she'd been framed. And then as soon as she was cleared, she'd found out the new mayor was under investigation and that the man she'd just started dating had been abducted right in front of her. "It doesn't make sense to me. Why do they want him?"

"Who did you say the new mayor is?" he asked. "Tad something?"

"Tad Howell. He was appointed by the town council, and by all accounts, he's a corrupt moron."

"Howell?" Warren asked with a growl. "Is his father Mason Howell?"

Iris frowned. "I'm not sure. Let me check." She quickly texted Gigi, letting her know she was fine and that she needed the name of Tad's father. It didn't take long before Gigi texted back that Sebastian had confirmed Tad's father was, in fact, Mason Howell.

"Dammit!" Warren rose and started pacing his kitchen. "Fuck!"

"What is it?" Iris asked as the fear she'd been successfully suppressing came roaring to the surface, making her heart race again. "How do you know the Howells?"

Warren paused, looked her straight in the eye, and said, "Mason Howell is the man who killed your father."

The breath left Iris's body, and her head swam. "What?"

Warren had already stormed out of the room.

Iris jumped up and followed him into the living room

where he was opening a false panel on the wall that revealed a large safe. "Warren?"

He glanced over his shoulder. "Your mother is in terrible danger. We have to get to her. Now."

"Do you know where she is?" Iris asked, her eyes wide as she watched him pull out a sword and a black amulet. After he strapped them both to his body, he reached in and grabbed a small, black velvet bag and tucked it into his pocket.

"I have a decent idea." Warren slammed the safe shut, stalked across the room, and yanked his door open. "Come on. We can't waste any more time."

Iris ran after him, but before he could head for his old Chevy, she pointed to her SUV and said, "We'll take my car. Gigi can drive while you explain."

He glanced at her modern, metallic blue vehicle and nodded once. "Yeah, okay. That's definitely less conspicuous."

Iris ran over and asked her friend to drive. Once Iris was in the backseat and Warren was in the front so that he could direct, she introduced them.

Gigi spared him a quick glance as she slammed the SUV into gear. "Nice to meet you, Warren."

"You, too, Gigi. Now step on it. There's no time to waste."

Gigi did as she was told while Iris texted the rest of the coven and told them to follow. When they agreed, no questions asked even though they could be headed into the lion's den, she let out a sigh of relief. Then Iris leaned forward between the seats and said, "Warren, I think you owe me an explanation."

He let out a humorless laugh. "Where do I start?"

"At the beginning. Why did Mason Howell kill my father?"

He winced. "You had to start there, didn't you?"

"Is there anywhere else to start?" she snapped, completely

out of patience. "Or do you want to tell me why you and my mother got divorced so suddenly and you didn't even say goodbye? Or why you two are still in touch and she knew exactly where to find you? What happened all those years ago, and why do you seem to know where she is right now?"

Warren rubbed his hands over his face and then raked his fingers through his hair. "Christ, what a fucked-up mess."

"You're telling me," Iris cried. "My entire life has fallen apart. My husband turned out to be a spineless criminal. I've lost my job. My mother and the new man in my life are both being held captive by the man who killed my father. Is there anything else that can go wrong?"

Warren turned to her, his face ashen. "Yes. They could take you next, and then the circle really would be complete."

Iris shook her head. "They had their opportunity to get me. They didn't. They took Kade instead. Besides, what would they even want with me? I'm nobody."

"That's where you're wrong, Iris. You're definitely someone. And now you've come into your father's power. They're just waiting for you to hand it over to them."

Gigi let out a gasp. "Her father's power?"

"That's... I don't understand," Iris said, frowning at both of them. "My father had power that they want?"

"You do know that it is rare for males to have significant power, right?" Gigi asked her.

"Yeah, I guess so," Iris said. "But my dad didn't have a lot of power."

"He did," Warren said. "A lot of it. And when he was with your mom, they were a very powerful couple."

"And they had an enemy in Howell?" Iris asked. "Why?"

"Mason and your dad had history. School rivalry. Bullshit stuff really. Or it was until your dad landed a mentorship with a powerful witch that Mason thought should be his." Warren shook his head. "That was the start of everything."

"So all of this goes back to Mason's ego being crushed?" Iris asked. "You're kidding, right?"

"I wish that was the issue." Warren rested his hand on the amulet he had strapped to his chest. "Your dad got in way too deep with his mentor and did some seriously questionable spells. Only he didn't know at the time that they targeted the Howell family."

"This mentor had a beef with the Howell's and used Iris's dad to curse them?" Gigi asked, her eyes wide.

"Pretty much exactly," Warren said. "Nate helped his mentor cast a curse that went terribly wrong. Mason's wife was a casualty. It was tragic, and it gutted Nate. He was instrumental in turning over evidence that ended with his mentor going to prison. But Mason never forgave Nate. Mason spent years sabotaging your parents until one night they got into it and Mason finally killed him. Only it wasn't an act of passion. He was trying to steal your father's power. Up until about twenty minutes ago, I thought he had. But it looks like you got it instead."

There was silence in the car as Iris took in his words. Iris had been there that afternoon when her father was killed. She'd didn't remember most of it. The incident was mostly a blank in her memory. But what she did know was that the moment her father had been shot, her entire body stiffened and she felt as if she'd been gut-punched by some sort of invisible force as her vision blurred. When it cleared, she'd dropped her Drumstick and run back to him. In later years when she thought about it, she just assumed she'd been in a state of shock. But what if it was more than that? What if that was the moment that her father's power had transferred to her?

Iris had been too young to really understand what was happening. But even now, when she thought of that moment, she still felt that bolt of energy that had nearly knocked her off her feet and taken her breath away. She doubted that without this conversation that she'd have ever considered that it might be magic that had slammed into her small body. The thought made her hands tingle as magic coated her palms.

"Whoa," she said, holding them up. "This never happens."

"It's getting stronger," Warren said. "That's a problem."

"Why?" Iris asked.

"It looks like the Howells are finally coming after the power they think is owed them. I'm sorry, Iris, but you're in danger."

"Again, if they wanted me, why didn't they take me when they had the chance?" she asked, still not at all convinced that Warren was right. She just didn't get why they'd take Kade and not her.

"It's because power freely given is more powerful than power that is stolen," Gigi said.

"That's insane. I'm not giving these people my power," Iris said defiantly. "Wouldn't that kill me?"

Warren's expression was grim when he said, "Yes. It would. But if you say no, they're likely to threaten to kill your mom and your boyfriend."

Pure rage rolled through Iris. She wanted to sputter her frustration. Scream until all the emotion was purged. "All of this that's happening right now with Tad is because of a feud between our parents? Does anyone else see how ridiculous that is?"

"A lot of people will do just about anything for power, Iris," Warren said. "That's what this is about."

"And a lot of people won't," she insisted. "Like you. There's a reason you left us, isn't there?"

He shrugged one shoulder.

"Warren?" she said, her voice hoarse. "Please, just tell me everything."

"I hate that I'm dumping all of this on you," he said.

"It's better to just do it now," she insisted.

He leaned his head back against the seat. "After your mother and I got together, they threatened her. I went after them and broke some laws. In the end, the only way to keep you both safe was to leave. So I did. For you and her and Nate. I thought me bowing out would protect you. That worked for a long time, but now..."

"Now what?" she asked, her eyes narrowed.

He turned back to look at her. "Now it's full-on war. I will not let anything happen to you or your mother. I owe you both and Nate that much."

"You still love her, don't you?" Iris asked, her voice going soft.

"Yes," he said simply. "I always have. Even before she was with Nate. But when they got together, I took a step back."

"Because you loved him, too," Iris said, her heart breaking for the only man she'd ever called stepfather, despite the fact that she'd had four others before him.

"I did." He let out a breath. "Nate was like a brother to me. One of the last conversations we ever had was him making me promise to look after you and your mom. I didn't do the best job, especially right after we lost Nate. But in the end, I did right by you both. And I will again today."

It was kind of nice to have a warrior, Iris thought. But even so, she was afraid that when push came to shove, she'd be the one making a choice: Sacrifice herself or lose her mother and Kade.

She knew what her choice would be every single time. Because just like her father and Warren, Iris would do anything to protect the ones she loved.

CHAPTER TWENTY-FOUR

"*T*his is it?" Iris peered through the windshield at what appeared to be an abandoned broken-down farmhouse in the middle of nowhere. They'd driven about an hour north of Warren's cabin, deep into the Northern California mountains. The last town they'd passed through was at least thirty miles away.

"See that dirt road?" Warren said, pointing to an area off to the left that was framed by overgrown brush and wild berry bushes.

"Yes," Gigi said as Iris's hands started to tingle with magic again.

"That's the back way in." Warren pulled a map up on his phone and pointed at another road that ran parallel to the one they were currently on. "That's the main entrance and is made to look like a logging road. An old truck is usually parked there, making it look like an active site so that no one thinks twice when cars go in and out."

"So they don't use this road?" Iris asked. The plan was for the coven to surround the building and cause a distraction while Warren snuck in to find Katheryn and Kade. But they had to get there undetected first.

"Not usually," Warren said.

"How do you know?" Gigi asked.

"Let's just say I've been keeping an eye on the Howells for years," Warren said with a scowl. "After everything they did to Iris's family, I wanted to make sure they were actually leaving them alone. It's been so long since all of that happened with Nate and then later when they were harassing us, that I haven't been paying as much attention the last few years. Otherwise, I would've already known they had Katheryn." His words came out in almost a growl. "I'm sorry," he said to Iris. "If I hadn't let my guard down, maybe it wouldn't have gotten this far."

"Like you said, it's been literally years," Iris said. "Over three decades. How could you have known they'd suddenly target me like this? If they really are after my power, how did they even know? It wasn't until after the curse on the town that I even started to notice a difference."

"It's a good question," Warren said. "One we'll surely find the answers to when we settle this once and for all." The fierceness etched all over his face both terrified and elated her. If there was one person she wanted on her side, it was Warren.

"Should I park here?" Gigi asked.

"No." Warren waved her on. "We don't want to be too far from the cars when we need to make our getaway."

Gigi slowly made her way along the road, and the closer they got, the more agitated Iris got. It wasn't nerves that had her jittery. It was the magic in the air. Her skin started to prickle, and she felt something like pressure building up beneath her skin.

"Park here," Warren ordered near a small alcove that was protected by a series of flowering bushes.

Once both cars were semi-hidden by the shrubbery, Warren waved the coven over and said, "They've got spells all over this place. Stay alert, and if we're lucky, we won't trip any. Once you're all in place, I'll get inside and find Katheryn. Then we'll—"

"And Kade," Iris interrupted. "I'm not leaving without him."

"Right. Katheryn and Kade," Warren said. "Once I have them out, you all take them back to the cars and get out. I'll keep them busy until you're clear."

"But what about you?" Iris asked, her heart racing. "We're not going to let you sacrifice yourself for the rest of us."

"Don't you worry about that," he said softly as he squeezed her hand. "I have no intention of letting them get the best of me. I'll find my way back. Trust me."

"I don't think—" Iris started, terrified that this was the last time that she'd see him.

"Stop thinking, Iris. I've been preparing for this for a very long time. Let's go get the people we love, okay?"

"Okay," she whispered, her heart shredded as she realized this man had sacrificed his whole life for her and her mother. He deserved better. She silently promised herself that she'd get him out one way or another.

"Let's go." Warren led the way down the dusty road, and when the large farmhouse came into view, he signaled to the coven to get into position. Then he slipped into the nearby forest and disappeared.

Iris took a deep breath and turned to her coven mates. "Are we ready?"

"I think so," Hope said. "Iris, you're with Gigi. If the two of you get a chance to combine your magic, it should be enough to ward off anything they manage to throw at you."

They'd decided to scatter around the house and create a

magical commotion. Everything but the house was fair game. With any luck, they'd create enough chaos that it would draw everyone out of the house, clearing the way for Warren to slip in unnoticed.

"Everyone be careful," said Hope, who'd taken on the unofficial role of leader. Iris decided it was because she planned events for a living. She was used to being in charge. "Watch out for magical land minds. And with any luck, we'll be out of here without breaking a sweat."

One could only hope.

The coven silently spread out around the farmhouse. Grace, Joy, and Carly snuck around to the back, while Hope, Gigi, and Iris took the front.

Iris's nerved were off the charts. The two people she cared about most were in that house. She couldn't stop herself from imagining what they'd gone through while being held captive. It made rage vibrate through her, and when the magic strumming under her skin intensified, she decided her anger was a good thing.

Hope raised her arms over her head, glanced at both Gigi and Iris. When they mirrored her, she nodded and all three let their magic fly.

Iris heard the wooden chairs on the porch splinter apart while the windows on a dilapidated old shed nearby shattered. She focused on an old rusting car that looked like it hadn't moved in over a decade. The metal screeched as she pried the fender off with just her mind. As the metal flew across the yard, it was so satisfying that she focused on the car again, and one by one, sheets of metal were ripped from the junker and hurled across the yard.

"What the fuck!" a man called as he bolted out the door with a gun in his hand.

"Take cover!" Hope ordered.

All three of the witches scattered. Iris found herself behind a redwood tree, her eyes wide as she watched two men spray bullets at the cars parked in the clearing. Bolts of white magic flew back at them, over and over, until one of the men was knocked across the yard and into a pillar on the house. He hung in the air against the pillar for a moment before he slid down and fell into a heap.

The other man called for backup and continued to spray bullets.

Iris stood there frozen, unsure of what to do. She could draw the gunman's fire, but it looked like Hope and Gigi were holding their own just fine.

Then the door opened, and Tad Howell stormed out, his face red as he yelled, "Can't you handle a couple of stupid witches? What the fuck is wrong with you?"

"Fuck off, Howell. I don't see you doing anything to help," the gunman said before he fired again.

Howell pulled out an amulet that looked an awful lot like the one Warren had taken from his safe and aimed it at the cars. The black stone that was mounted at the end of a cane glowed red. A loud boom rumbled through the air, making the ground shake. Immediately after, random areas of the ground around the house started exploding as if magical bombs were going off.

Iris held on to the redwood and let out a cry when one of the magical bombs went off a few feet from her.

"You!" Tad pointed at her and sprinted in her direction, the amulet aimed right at her. "If it wasn't for you, no one would be investigating us!"

Iris wasn't sure what that meant. Was he talking about the Magical Task Force? Or some other agency? Either way, she was quite certain that he had no one to blame but himself. "Maybe you should have thought of that before you cursed Premonition Pointe," Iris spat.

"You bitch!" He lunged at her, the amulet sputtering with magic that went haywire and bounced off the tree, leaving a burn mark.

That rage was back, and Iris flung herself at him, grabbing hold of his arms and taking them both down. Tad convulsed as the magic that had been brimming just beneath the surface shot out of her hands and into him. His eyes rolled into the back of his head, and drool trickled out of his open mouth.

Iris immediately jumped up, afraid that she was killing the man. The sounds of magic and gunshots still rang through the air, but where she and Tad had landed, they were hidden from the action. Iris just prayed that all her coven mates were safe and that Warren had found her mother and Kade. She knew she should get back to the fight, but what she needed were answers. And she wasn't leaving until she pried them out of Tad.

The man at her feet stilled, and when his eyes came back into focus, he stared up at her, hatred streaming off him in waves. "You never deserved to be mayor," he said through gritted teeth.

Iris let out a humorless laugh. "Seriously? I'm the one who was elected. You were appointed by what I can only assume is a corrupt city council."

"Your dad killed my mother and ruined my life," he said. The coldness in his gaze made Iris shiver. "It was time to ruin yours."

"So that's what all this is about? Revenge?" Iris was aware that he hadn't moved a muscle since he'd come out of the seizure she'd caused with her magic. Wary that he was trying to fool her into complacency, she crouched down but left enough room that he couldn't just reach out and grab her. Then she picked up the amulet that had fallen by his feet and tucked it behind her.

"Not entirely, but it was a really good bonus." He closed his eyes and moaned when he tried to push himself into a sitting position. "Your father got my mother killed. Do you have any idea what it was like growing up without her?"

"Probably about the same as it was growing up without my father," she shot back. "That wasn't enough revenge for you?"

Iris grabbed the amulet and jabbed the wooden end to his chest, forcing him back down. "Why else did you get me pushed out and frame me for that curse on Premonition Pointe? To get rid of me to make it easier to run drugs through town?"

"Of course it was," he hissed. "You're not that stupid, are you?"

No, she wasn't. "You won't get away with this. You know that, right?"

"We will if you get slapped with assault and battery along with a trespassing charge." Tad shifted his focus to the amulet. "I can't believe that thing misfired. It really would've been poetry if the weapon used to kill you was your father's own amulet."

Iris jerked the amulet up to take a look at it, but before she could, Tad reached out, trying to grab it from her.

Dammit! He'd been baiting her to get the upper hand. Without any effort from her, magic poured into the amulet and shot down the cane, sending a bolt right into his chest. He fell, listless and breathing heavily. "Looks like the amulet was returned to its rightful owner. Did your father steal this from him the day he killed my dad?"

"Warriors deserve their spoils," he spat out as if they were living in the fifteenth century and pillaging was the norm.

"Looks like I've reclaimed this one then," she said and had a sudden image of the amulet Warren also carried. She could only assume they'd gotten them at the same time and had fought side by side on numerous occasions. They had been best friends after all. "Move again, and I'll end you," Iris warned.

"Good luck trying," he said, his lips curving up into a self-satisfied smile as he looked over her shoulder.

Just as Iris turned to see what or who he was looking at, she heard her ex's voice. "Dammit, Iris. Why didn't you just leave when I told you to?"

"Because I—oomph!" Her head exploded in pain just before her world went black.

CHAPTER TWENTY-FIVE

*I*ris woke to a splitting headache. She rolled to her side and groaned as the world spun. She blinked gingerly, causing her vision to blur and her stomach to lurch. Oh gods, she was going to vomit, wasn't she?

"If you need to puke, do it here," Tom said, his tone void of any emotion.

"Tom?" she asked, confused. Why was he acting so cold?

"Of course it's Tom. Did you think it was someone else who knocked you out?"

"What?" She brought her hands up to steady her head just as the flashbacks started flickering in her mind. Finding Warren, learning that he'd left to keep her safe, and then finding themselves at the farmhouse in the middle of a magical battle so that they could save Kade and her mother. Finally, she heard the words of her ex right before she'd been knocked out.

Why didn't you leave when I told you to?

"Why are you doing this?" she asked him. She heard the sadness in her question and wondered, not for the first time, why he'd gotten involved with drug dealers. They'd had a nice

211

life, or so she'd thought. Maybe it wasn't the most exciting or passionate, but they'd been friends and comfortable with each other. It wasn't a life she ever wanted to go back to, but it couldn't have been so bad that it made him decide to risk everything he had to help distribute drugs that had actually been killing people.

He barked out a laugh. "Why? Do you think I ever had a choice?"

Iris's vision finally cleared. She glanced around and noted that they were in some sort of hunting cabin. There were dead animal heads on the walls along with vintage rifles. Were they still on the same property, or had Tom taken her somewhere else? She focused on the man she'd shared her life with for a decade and a half. She didn't even recognize him anymore. "Of course you had a choice. You still have choices."

"Not any good ones." He waved toward the back of the cabin. "Tad is dead. If I don't do something, they'll kill me, too."

Iris gasped. "Tad's dead?"

"He tried to take you so they could harvest your magic. I couldn't have that. If that happens, the Howell crime family will be unstoppable. So it's up to me to figure this out." He paced back and forth while flexing his fingers as if to work out some kinks.

"You killed him?" she asked again, still not quite sure she could process the information.

"Yes. I said I did, didn't I?" He was agitated now, and Iris was starting to wonder if he was doing drugs himself. That would explain a few things.

She wanted to know how he'd killed Tad, but she just couldn't bring herself to say the words. The situation was so surreal, she feared she was having trouble staying grounded in reality.

"You really shouldn't have come here, Iris," he said, pausing to stare at her. "Why in the world didn't you just leave town? There's nothing in Premonition Pointe for you anymore."

Iris managed to push herself up into a sitting position on the cracked leather couch without vomiting. *Thank everything holy for that.* Tom's words kept running over and over in her head. Did he really think there was nothing for her in Premonition Pointe? Even if she hadn't started a relationship with Kade, she'd always loved Premonition Pointe. Tom should know that. It was her place. The first time she'd stepped foot in the town, she'd just felt settled. Right. Like she belonged. Even without any friends or connections to anyone, she'd known the town was where she was meant to be.

"Did you ever even know me at all, Tom?" she asked.

"What's that supposed to mean?" His dark eyes flashed with irritation. "Of course I know you. You gave all of your energy to people you barely knew, leaving nothing left for me or our marriage. There was nothing more important to you than the power of being mayor. It took precedence over everything, including our anniversary, which was ruined three years in a row because of town business. I know that you never really loved me and the only reason we were together was for your image. You, Iris Hartsen, are the most selfish person I've ever met."

Iris's mouth dropped open in shock at his outburst. She was immediately defensive and could've come up with any number of barbs to throw at him about how he'd prioritized his business over the years. How he'd never been there for any of her milestones or accomplishments. Yet, she'd gone to every dinner party he'd arranged when he was wining and dining his business contacts. Or how she'd set him up with suppliers and retail outlets every chance she got to help support him. But mostly she was just hurt.

Some of Tom's accusations had truth to them. It was probably true that she'd prioritized her job over the time she spent with Tom. And that because the passion had faded, she hadn't paid him as much attention over the years. But that was a two-way street.

"You know what bothers me most?" Tom asked.

"What?" she asked quietly, not at all sure she wanted to know anything else he had to say.

"You never even told me about your father or that you were there the day he died. All you ever said was that he died when you were young. But you told that jackass Kade?" The ire in his tone made Iris flinch. "We were married for years, and you didn't even trust me enough to share that trauma. Our marriage was a complete sham, Iris. It's no wonder I had an affair!"

Oh, that did it. Iris stood and placed her hands on her hips. "You will not blame me for your indiscretions. I was always faithful to you, and you know it. Maybe I never shared because you obviously weren't a safe person. A safe loving person would never install nanny cams to spy on their wife. You're vile, Tom. And I can't believe I wasted so many years with you!"

His expression went completely blank again, and he shrugged before he turned and opened the refrigerator. A second later, he pulled out two bottles of water and threw one at her.

Iris caught it easily, but made no move to drink it. She was far too keyed up to do anything other than glare at him. If looks could kill, he'd have combusted already. "Just tell me why you're doing this. Why you're mixed up with these people and why you're holding me here."

"I told you, they forced me into this. If you'd left town when I asked you to, I'd have been out of this shithole drug ring. You know, I never intended to be a part of this, but Yasmeen dragged me into it, and now here we are." He walked over and sat down on the couch.

Because he was talking and she recognized that his guard was down, she sat too, hoping that she'd get the entire story.

"Can you just start at the beginning? Help me understand, and then we can find a way out of this," she said, pleading in her tone. "We cared about each other once, Tom. Can't we just help each other now?"

He searched her gaze for a moment before leaning back into the couch and pressing a hand to his eyes. "It started with Yasmeen. It was a cocktail party, and one thing led to another. After we slept together, she blackmailed me into being an Ashe distributor."

Iris expected to be angry or jealous, but she just felt pity for the man. He'd been stupid, and there was no excuse for the way he'd acted. But she'd already accepted that their marriage had its problems, and he wasn't the only one at fault. "And then when Yasmeen went to prison, I thought you cut a deal with the prosecutors. Why didn't you walk away then?"

"I tried. The Howells wouldn't let me. They said if I gathered info on you, they'd cut me loose. Only they never did, and I just kept getting in deeper. Then when you were arrested, they told me if I got you to leave Premonition Pointe, that I'd be free too." He buried his face in his hands and let out a groan. "If only you'd listened to me then."

"But I didn't," Iris said, pressing a hand to her gut.

"No. You didn't. And then we learned that you suddenly had power, and Tad over there"—Tom waved an impatient hand—"decided that he was going to kill you in order to take your power and increase his. Do you know what would've happened to Premonition Pointe then?"

Iris nodded. Her mouth had gone dry. She knew that they'd wanted to kill her, but to hear Tom say it in such a matter-of-fact way had left her shaking. Iris opened the water she was still holding and took a long swig.

Tom watched her intently, not saying anything.

"What?" she asked.

"Nothing." But he continued to watch her closely. After a moment, he said, "You never thanked me for getting rid of Tad for you."

"What?" Iris's mind started to get fuzzy, and she squinted at him, knowing she should be upset by what he'd just said, but she just couldn't quite put together why.

"He would have killed you and then used your power to destroy Premonition Pointe. But because of me, your precious town will live on and be just fine. Surely your coven will watch over it."

"I'll be there." Her words slurred, and her limbs were starting to feel heavy. Was she experiencing concussion symptoms?

"Oh, no you won't, love," Tom said, placing a hand on her arm. "You really didn't think I could let you live, did you? I need to tell the Howells that someone killed Tad. It sure as hell isn't going to be me. And the bonus is that getting rid of you now means I'll get your power *and* your father's amulet, and no one else will make me their bitch. So thank you for this one last gift."

"Tom?" she croaked out, her throat starting to close up. "You poisoned me." It wasn't a question. It was a statement.

"No one ever said you were dumb." He got up and moved out of her sightline.

Iris's limbs were heavy, and her brain was moving slow. She knew that if she didn't get help soon, she really would die.

Panic flooded her, and she opened her mouth to call for help, but nothing came out. Tears filled her eyes and hope fled.

Stupid. Stupid. Stupid.

Of all the ways to be taken out, it was going to be by her jackass ex? What would her mom say?

Her heart cracked when she thought of how devastated her mother would be. She'd blame herself for not being there with an antidote.

Antidote. The word flashed in her mind like a neon sign.

Iris's breath caught, and although her fingers were barely moving, she fumbled with the latch on the crossbody bag she'd put on earlier that day. The bottle she needed was right where she'd left it. Sweat broke out over her skin as she frantically tried to get the top off. Her fingers weren't working right, and her time was running out.

There was movement behind her, and she knew it was now or never. If Tom caught her with the antidote now, her chance at survival would be snatched from her forever.

"What the fuck is that?" Tom cried. Footsteps boomed on the wood floors, indicating he was coming.

Iris ripped the cap off and downed the contents of the potion her mother had insisted she'd need right before she'd stormed out the day before. The effects were immediate. Her head cleared, and her vision came into sharp focus just in time to register that Tom's fist was coming right at her. Iris threw herself on the floor and rolled expertly to her feet. She was elated to realize that the self-defense classes she'd taken years ago had paid off.

"What the hell was in that bottle?" he demanded as he squared off with her.

"The antidote. It turns out my mother has the gift of sight and anticipated that I'd need it."

His mouth dropped open before it twisted into a scowl.

"Oh, I guess that pisses you off, too, that you didn't know the extent of my mother's power. Too bad for you. It turns out I didn't trust you with a lot."

He lunged for her, but she was ready for him and kicked a foot out, immediately connecting with his knee. He went down with a cry as he clutched at his leg.

"You're pathetic," Iris said right before she stomped down on his knee one more time for good measure.

Tom grunted and rolled away from her, but she wasn't done. All the built-up rage she'd tried to put behind her over the last few months since she'd found out about his extracurricular activities came roaring back and joined with her utter contempt of the man who'd just tried to kill her for his own gain.

"You're a complete waste of oxygen," she said through clenched teeth and kicked him as hard as she could in the gut. Then she willed herself to think rationally. Beating his ass might be satisfying, but what she really needed to do was secure him so that he was no longer a threat until law enforcement could come take him away.

It didn't take long for her to find some zip ties in the small kitchen. They were larger than she was used to seeing, and she couldn't help but wonder if they'd been purchased for the explicit purpose of securing a prisoner's hands and feet.

Considering the circumstances of her visit to the cabin, she wouldn't be surprised.

"They'll still come after you," Tom warned as she forced his wrists into the ties.

"Maybe. But you already killed Tad for me, so that's one less I have to worry about." Once she was certain he wasn't going anywhere, she moved to the front window and peeked out. There were trees everywhere and not a soul in sight.

They had to have gotten there somehow. After searching Tom's pockets, she found a set of keys and then walked outside to find a white van parked next to the cabin.

Freedom.

Iris cast a glance at the cabin, wondering if she should leave Tom there. It didn't take long for her to decide that she could never move him on her own. There wasn't much of a choice.

With her decision made, she climbed into the van, determined to find Kade and her mother and the rest of the coven. But as soon as she shoved the key into the ignition, a familiar gray SUV pulled into the clearing.

Iris spotted Kade in the driver's seat and immediately jumped out of the van, running toward him, waving her hands in elated relief.

The SUV jerked to a stop and in the next second, Kade was out of the car and Iris was hurling herself into his arms.

"Iris," he said, his voice thick with emotion. "We thought we'd lost you."

A sob got caught in her throat before she forced out, "I thought the same about you."

Iris didn't know how long they stood there holding each other. It could have been seconds or hours. All she knew was that she had the one man she'd ever really trusted in her arms and they were both safe.

"Honey?" Katheryn's voice finally permeated Iris's Kade-bubble.

Iris pulled back and felt relief rush through her body. Immediately she let go of Kade and threw her arms around her mother. "Thank you. Thank you. Thank you."

"For what?" Katheryn asked, running her hand over the back of Iris's head, soothing her.

"You saved my life. The potion. Tom poisoned me. You knew and you saved me by making the antidote."

"That fucker. I'll kill him myself," Katheryn growled in her mama bear voice.

"Not if I do it first," Warren said from right behind them.

Iris glanced at him and let go of her mother. "Is it over? Does the Magical Task Force have them in custody?"

"They do. Another unit is on their way here now that we know you're here," he said. His brow furrowed and his expression darkened when he asked, "What happened here?"

"Tom killed Tad and abducted me," she said, her voice surprisingly steady. It fortified her and she reached out for Kade as she added, "Tom poisoned me, but thanks to Mom, I had an antidote. I managed to get it down before the poison took me out. After that, I kicked Tom's ass and tied him up. I was on my way to find the rest of you when you showed up, saving me the trouble."

"Holy shit, Iris. Your dad always did say you were full of moxie. Remind me to always pick you first when I need someone on my team," Warren said with a huge grin.

Iris smiled back at him. "You will if you know what's good for you."

He laughed and pulled her into a hug. "It's damned good seeing you again, Moxie girl."

"You too," she said on a happy sob. "How did you guys find me?"

"Tracking device," Katheryn said. "I put one in your bag the day I made your potion."

Iris couldn't even be mad. She was certain the tracker was a result of another vision, and at that moment all she felt was grateful.

The rest of the coven gathered around them and chattered about how they'd kicked ass and taken names. Iris would still need to talk to the Magical Task Force, but it was looking like the Howell family business was likely done in Premonition Pointe and out of business for good.

CHAPTER TWENTY-SIX

*I*ris took a sip of wine while she waited for her date at her new favorite restaurant. There was a slight breeze from the ocean, and the patio was full of tourists. As it turned out, Tad had cast the curse that had banished all the tourists, and when he died, the curse died with him. As near as Iris could piece together, he'd done it for three reasons: to bilk the business owners for a thousand dollars each to pay off debts he owed when business deals went bad, to frame Iris and make her life hell because her father was partially to blame for his mother's death all those years ago, and lastly, so that when he lifted the curse, he'd be seen as the town hero.

It was too bad for Tad that he got none of those things, and everyone who worked for the family business had been arrested and held without bail. Because they'd tried to steal Iris's magic, they were considered too risky for society.

Now the town was full of tourists again, and Iris was enjoying the warm summer sun as she watched Kade wind his way through the tables toward her. Iris lit up from the inside like she always did when she saw him. It had been a month since the showdown with the Howells, and ever since then Iris had spent every night with Kade. She kept expecting the excited vibes of the new relationship to fade, but they hadn't yet. And in fact, she was starting to feel like she was settling into them. Her heart was always fuller when he was around.

"Hey, gorgeous," Kade said as he leaned down to kiss her cheek. "How was your day?"

"Good. I had a meeting with the members of the city council." After the Howell scandal hit the papers, a couple of the city council members had resigned in disgrace, and the remaining councilors had filled those interim slots with respected members of the community until a regular election could be held. Both of the members who resigned were being investigated for fraud, but Iris wasn't sure how deep they were into the scandal. It appeared they'd accepted campaign funds from the Howells and lobbied for Tad to pay back the favor. The rest just hadn't done their due diligence when appointing Tad or ousting Iris. They'd been too concerned about appearances instead of who actually was a good fit for the job.

Kade took a seat across from her and raised his eyebrows in surprise. "Really? What did the council want?"

"They want me to be interim mayor until the next election," Iris said with a smug smile.

"Oh, wow," Kade said with a grimace. "You're not thinking of taking it, are you?"

Iris's smile faded. "Would it be an issue if I did?"

"What?" he asked, sounding surprised by the question. "Of course not. I was just thinking about the way they treated you. It's hard for me to imagine you heading back into that sort of situation. That's all. You deserve all the respect. Not to be tossed out because someone you know did something beyond your control."

Iris reached over and threaded her fingers through his. "That's exactly how I feel. To be fair, they did apologize, and I think most of them meant it. But still... I think I can do better things for Premonition Pointe than be the mayor. Something more tangible and hands-on."

"Like be the director of that nonprofit we talked about?" he asked hopefully.

Iris gave him a brilliant smile. "The one that my boyfriend is dying to set up as soon as he finds someone to run it? That nonprofit?"

His eyes glinted with amusement. "That would be the one."

"Yes. If you still want me, then I'm in."

Kade got to his feet and pulled her up into a hug. "I think you're going to be amazing. Thank you for trusting me."

"No, thank you for... everything." She held on for a few seconds longer before taking her seat and ordering a round of margaritas.

Iris had been given many options for new job opportunities over the past month. Everything from the mayorship to regional vice president of a major new-age retailer. She'd interviewed and carefully weighed the pros and cons of each and every one. But the only one that excited her was the idea Kade had thrown at her during one of their weekly hikes. He wanted to use some of the money he'd made to open a nonprofit that would help seed small businesses. The awards would be need-based, and the business plans had to pass Iris's approval before they were funded.

The moment Kade had mentioned it, Iris had known that's what she wanted to do. The work checked all of her boxes. She got to help Premonition Pointe grow, use her gift for business ideas, and help those who could use a hand up. Her salary wasn't going to be nearly as impressive as many of the other job offers, but she didn't care. This was the one that would feed her soul. Besides, she didn't need a boatload of money for herself. She already had everything she needed. A boyfriend who she'd fallen head over heels for, her coven who'd become her ride-or-die friends, and a new start with her mother and Warren. And now she had her dream job. Not to mention BeeBee, the sweetest, most lovable dog on the planet, had decided Iris was her favorite person.

"We made it! Finally," Katheryn said as she slid into the seat next to Iris.

Warren was close behind and sat across from her beside Kade.

The waiter appeared with their drinks, and Katheryn gladly took a long sip before sitting back and letting out a contented sigh. "You would not believe the traffic out there."

"It's great isn't it?" Iris said, smiling at them.

"Sure. For the town, but not so much for me when I'm already late for lunch." Despite her grumbling, there was an ease to her mother that Iris hadn't really ever seen in her before. She was relaxed and... happy. It made Iris's heart swell. In the past month, she and her mother had talked a lot. After a lot of honesty and even more tears, Iris had finally forgiven her for the upheaval of her childhood. And Iris had apologized for always shutting her mother out. There were still times when Katheryn was overbearing and thought everything should be her way, but it was a work in progress. Iris was better able to draw her boundaries, and Katheryn was better at respecting them.

"We have some news," Warren said.

Katheryn let out a giggle.

A giggle of all things, Iris thought and couldn't help her own chuckle. Who was this person who called herself Iris's mother? Iris loved seeing all of the new sides of her.

"Well, don't leave us in suspense. What is it?" Kade asked.

Katheryn shoved her hand out, showing off a pink diamond that was surrounded by a tasteful ring of white diamonds. "Warren and I are getting remarried."

Iris's eyes widened, and then she burst into happy tears. "Really?" she asked, although she didn't really need for them to answer. Warren hadn't left Katheryn's side since the day he'd carried her from the Howell home. And the love between them was obvious.

"Really," Warren said, taking Katheryn's other hand and kissing her palm. "Is that okay with you?"

Iris pressed a hand to her heart. "Of course it's okay. This calls for a toast." She raised her margarita glass and waited for them to do the same. Then she said, "To true love and never giving up on the future, no matter how much time has passed."

Katheryn and Warren smiled shyly at each other and then sipped their drinks.

After they chattered for a bit, Kade cleared his throat. "I have news, too. Or at least an update."

They all turned to him. "Just before I came to lunch, the new DA called. Tom took a deal. He turned state's witness just like he did last time, but he's not getting off with probation. He'll be serving time. Lots of it. The charges were just too serious. He's looking at a long stretch in prison."

Iris thought she'd feel vindicated when she heard the news. She'd known Tom wasn't going to walk like he did last time, and she was grateful the Magical Task Force had stepped in. That action had brought attention to the corruption in Premonition Pointe and caused a massive investigation. Many people went to jail. Others cut deals and quietly walked away.

The one surprise was Julie. In the end, they'd found out that Julie was the one who'd cleansed the magic from Iris's yard. She hadn't meant to frame her former boss. She was trying to protect her. Julie hadn't been sure who was responsible for the curse, but she'd hated Tad and wanted to help Iris in any way she could. Her misguided actions had landed her with probation and a stern warning from the MTF agent. Iris had forgiven her and hoped that with time, she and Julie could be friends again.

"Well, good riddance," Katheryn said. "I never did like that weasel Tom. He was never good enough for my baby." Katheryn put her arm around Iris and pulled her in for a sideways hug.

"Thanks, Mom. I guess making bad choices runs in the family," she said with a sad chuckle.

"Maybe, but we've got two great ones now. And that's all that matters." She kissed Iris on the top of the head, and Iris couldn't remember ever being so happy.

CHAPTER TWENTY-SEVEN

*C*arly Preston grabbed a glass of champagne and stared up at the brilliant stars in the sky. Inside her beachside home, there were A-listers celebrating the wrap of yet another movie. She'd just starred as the grandmother in a teen drama that was both surprisingly funny and full of so much heart that even Carly had cried at the bittersweet ending. It was the type of film that would likely win awards.

After making the rounds and playing the gracious starlet, Carly had congratulated the young actors who were likely on the verge of stardom and then quietly slipped outside so that the pull in her gut would finally ease.

The nighttime stars had always called to Carly. Since an early age, she'd always found herself outside, listening and waiting for whatever message they had for her. It wasn't until after her eighteenth birthday that they'd taken on a bigger, more significant role, indicating that she was about to get a visit from the beyond.

The French doors opened, and Carly stifled a sigh at the interruption until she saw Joy, Gigi, and Iris coming toward her. The women of the Premonition Pointe coven were her favorite people. Carly had been blessed with many friends over the years. She'd been lucky in her life to have many people care about her, or at least care enough about her career to care about her. But these ladies were different. There was a real connection between them, and Carly was grateful that they'd welcomed her into their circle, not because she was a famous actress, but because they actually liked her *despite* her fame.

Joy, Carly's former co-star on another movie, came and sat next to her. "Escaped again, I see," she teased.

Carly chuckled. "Looks like you three are following in my footsteps."

Iris sighed and leaned against the deck railing. "There is a guy in there who can't stop asking me questions about the Howells. I think he wants to write a screenplay." She grimaced. "I get that it's an interesting story, but if he asks to see my dad's amulet one more time, I think I'm going to curse him with it."

"You're not going to curse anyone with that amulet," Gigi said with a shake of her head. "That's not your style. You're more likely to slip them some sort of potion that makes them want to watch Netflix and chill."

"I thought Netflix and chill was code for a hookup," Carly said. "Maybe you can sell that potion in the adult toy stores."

Iris threw her head back and laughed. "Now that's an idea. I probably wouldn't slip them something that makes them want to bone down, but something to make them chill out really is kinda more my style. I just want everyone to be happy. Is that so wrong?"

"Nope," Joy said, smiling at her. "It's one of the things we love about you."

Iris smiled at her and looked so content that Carly was almost jealous. Had she ever felt that way? Carly wasn't sure. She liked her life. Hell, she loved it at times, but contentment wasn't a feeling she was intimately familiar with. There was always something just out of reach, and she'd never figured out what that might be.

"Anyway," Iris said, "I'm not going to be showing that guy my amulet. It's going to stay right where it is in my new potions studio. I like having it there. It makes me feel closer to my dad."

Gigi reached over and squeezed her hand, and something like understanding passed between them. The two of them had started working together on some new product lines that were sold at Skyler's shop in town. They were a good fit with both of them being earth witches. Because Carly was also skilled with herbs and potions, she felt a deeper connection to the two of them than most of the other witches in the coven. She loved them all, especially Joy, who'd been instrumental in helping her find her niece when she'd been abducted a while back, but it wasn't that same bone-deep connection that she had to people who shared gifts similar to her own. She just understood them on a molecular level.

Maybe one day she'd figure out how to let her guards down and let them know just how much they meant to her.

"Let me guess. The guy who keeps bugging you is Barry Barstow?" Carly asked with a wrinkle of her nose.

"Yes." Iris said. "He's kind of smarmy."

Carly laughed. "A lot of Hollywood types are. If you ever decide you want that story told, let me know. I'll put you in touch with people who'll treat you right and do the story justice. And the media would bring a lot of attention to the nonprofit you and Kade are starting."

"Hmm. I hadn't thought of it like that," Iris said. "It's

something to mull over. Still, I'm not sure I'll ever want to do that, but I'll let you know if I change my mind. Thank you."

"Of course. Anything for you and your coven mates," Carly said, meaning it.

"*Our* coven mates," Joy corrected her. "You're one of us now. You know that, right?"

"I didn't know I'd been initiated into the club," Carly said with a teasing smile. "I thought that would come with a streaking session on the beach or something." The words were light and playful, but Carly's heart had swelled with emotion. These were the kinds of friendships that were lifechanging. The clarity of the moment was not lost on her. She'd found her circle, and she intended to hold on with both hands. She just hoped she didn't fuck it up somehow, like she'd done all those years ago.

"Hell week starts the day after Labor Day," Joy said. "You'll get the schedule delivered by half-naked men, under the light of the full moon just before midnight the day before."

The group cracked up, and Carly just grinned at them, feeling a twinge of that contentment that had always eluded her.

The French doors opened again. This time Kade poked his head out. "Hey, Iris, can you come in for a minute? There's someone I want you to talk to."

"Sure thing." She excused herself, and Joy and Gigi went with her, indicating they needed more champagne.

Immediately, the stars called to Carly again. She let herself focus, waiting for the visit she knew was coming. The world around her started to fade. The slight breeze disappeared along with the gentle crashing of the waves below. There was nothing but darkness and the brilliant diamonds overhead.

Then it happened. There was a ripple in reality, and her

twin sister, the one she'd lost just before their eighteenth birthday, appeared beside her.

"Hi, sis," Caydence said.

Carly turned to her sister, who was trapped in time, and smiled through her tears at the fresh-faced girl with long blond hair and brilliant green eyes. It didn't happen often, but Carly cherished the moments when her sister visited her. "Hey, yourself. Long time no see."

Caydence shrugged. "Your life has been pretty boring for the last few years. You know, you should really live more. This making movies thing is cool and all, but you're not really happy."

"I know." There was no sense in denying it. She couldn't hide anything from her twin. "If you're here, that means something's about to change, right?" Every time her twin had shown up throughout the years, something significant had come right after. It was as if Caydence was trying to prepare her or something.

"Yep. It's a doozy, too."

Carly grimaced at her. "That sounds ominous. Why are you always so mysterious? Details would be helpful, you know."

Her sister smiled sweetly at her. "Where would the fun be in that?"

"Why do you torture me?" Carly asked, but there was humor there. Over the years, Carly had accepted that these visits were never to give her the answers to whatever was coming. They were to offer support and love from the one person Carly had ever completely trusted.

"I miss you," Caydence said, her tone wistful.

"I miss you, too."

They sat in silence, just enjoying being in the presence of each other the way they had countless times as children.

Finally, Caydence turned to Carly and gave her the message she'd come to give. "Changes are coming, Carly. Big changes. And you need to be open to them."

"What changes?" Carly asked, but she knew Caydence wouldn't answer.

Caydence reached over, squeezed Carly's hand, and then disappeared back into the universe.

Carly sat there, letting the pain of losing Caydence wash over her, through her, until the pain in her heart eased. Then she got up and went back inside.

No one paid much attention to her as she slowly made her way toward her coven members, who were gathered together near the foyer. But just before she got to them, she felt a pull, an uncontrollable instinct to head for her front door.

Frowning to herself, she moved toward the door. And just before she reached for the doorknob, a knock sounded from the other side.

Her heart raced, and Carly knew that whoever stood on the other side of her door was the change her sister had warned her about. There was no turning away from it. There was nothing to do but face it head on. Taking a deep breath, she opened the door, and her jaw dropped when she saw the man standing on her porch.

"Hi, Carly," Jeremiah Vance said, his eyes tired and wary.

"Jeremiah?" Carly breathed out. She hadn't seen him in over thirty years. Not since the week after they'd both lost their siblings in that terrible boating accident and he'd very publicly blamed her. Besides her sister Caydence, his brother Zane had been her very best friend in the entire world. Losing them both had nearly broken her. "What are you doing here?"

He swallowed hard. "It's about Zane. I think he's alive, and I need your help."

Witches of Keating Hollow:
Soul of the Witch
Heart of the Witch
Spirit of the Witch
Dreams of the Witch
Courage of the Witch
Love of the Witch
Power of the Witch
Essence of the Witch
Muse of the Witch
Vision of the Witch
Waking of the Witch

Witches of Christmas Grove:
A Witch For Mr. Holiday
A Witch For Mr. Christmas
A Witch For Mr. Winter

Premonition Pointe Novels:
Witching For Grace
Witching For Hope
Witching For Joy
Witching For Clarity
Witching For Moxie
Witching For Kismet

Jade Calhoun Novels:
Haunted on Bourbon Street
Witches of Bourbon Street
Demons of Bourbon Street
Angels of Bourbon Street
Shadows of Bourbon Street
Incubus of Bourbon Street
Bewitched on Bourbon Street
Hexed on Bourbon Street
Dragons of Bourbon Street

Pyper Rayne Novels:
Spirits, Stilettos, and a Silver Bustier
Spirits, Rock Stars, and a Midnight Chocolate Bar
Spirits, Beignets, and a Bayou Biker Gang
Spirits, Diamonds, and a Drive-thru Daiquiri Stand
Spirits, Spells, and Wedding Bells

Ida May Chronicles:
Witched To Death
Witch, Please
Stop Your Witchin'

Crescent City Fae Novels:

Influential Magic
Irresistible Magic
Intoxicating Magic

Last Witch Standing:
Bewitched by Moonlight
Soulless at Sunset
Bloodlust By Midnight
Bitten At Daybreak

Witch Island Brides:
The Wolf's New Year Bride
The Vampire's Last Dance
The Warlock's Enchanted Kiss
The Shifter's First Bite

Destiny Novels:
Defining Destiny
Accepting Fate

Wolves of the Rising Sun:
Jace
Aiden
Luc
Craved
Silas
Darien
Wren

Black Bear Outlaws:
Cyrus
Chase

Cole

Bayou Springs Alien Mail Order Brides:
Zeke
Gunn
Echo

ABOUT THE AUTHOR

New York Times and USA Today bestselling author, Deanna Chase, is a native Californian, transplanted to the slower paced lifestyle of southeastern Louisiana. When she isn't writing, she is often goofing off with her husband in New Orleans or playing with her two shih tzu dogs. For more information and updates on newest releases visit her website at deannachase.com.